THE THREAD OF THE INFINITE

Proudly published by Snowbooks
Copyright © 2019 Various
The authors assert the moral right to be identified as the author of this work. All rights reserved.

Snowbooks Ltd
info@snowbooks.com
www.snowbooks.com

British Library Cataloguing in Publication Data.
A catalogue record for this book is available from the British Library.

First published August 2019

Paperback 978-1-911390-71-8
eBook 978-1-911390-72-5

THE THREAD OF THE INFINITE
Tales of Industrial Horror

Compiled & Edited By
Dean M. Drinkel

For Romain

"What happened between those two beings?
Nothing. They were adoring one another."
– Victor Hugo, *Les Miserables*

"The Beautiful is always strange."
– Charles Baudelaire

Contents

FOREWORD	7
INTRODUCTION	13
In the City of Concrete Dandelions	
Cate Gardner	16
A Night In The Bone Factory	
Adrian Cole	30
Slippery When Wet	
Marie O'Regan	54
The Harvest	
Phil Sloman	68
Transcending Nature	
Stephanie Ellis	98
Idle Hands Are Grist To His Mill	
Adrian Chamberlin	120
Dull Den	
Allen Ashley	153
March of the Midnight Crow	
Leah Crowley	180
A Prospect Greater Than The Sea	
Dean M. Drinkel	189
BIOGRAPHIES	225

FOREWORD

A (Really Bad) History Of Horror To Get You Up To Speed

Twenty-three years ago now I turned up for my first meeting with my PhD supervisor, trying to convince him that rather than going down the same avenue of Gothic literature I really wanted to examine the influence of region - and specifically industrialised areas - upon the kind of fiction they put out. You see, I'd got a bee in my particular bonnet that the hotbeds of horror were all key traditional mining, shipbuilding and steel towns. If you looked at a map, our 1990s British horror writers seemed to be clustered around Newcastle, Liverpool, Leeds, Birmingham and the like, and it fascinated me. What was it about these regions that nurtured horror writers? What was the link between the dehumanising machines, the gigantic behemoths of concrete, iron and steel that dominated the landscapes, and those deep-seated fears that are rooted in our basic animal instincts? Was there even a link, or was it just a purely random quirk of the time, because there were exceptions, so for every Ramsey Campbell of Clive Barker putting Liverpool on the map, there was a Chris Fowler working out of London.

I've always believed there are primarily two kinds of horror - one where the enemy is some unknown, some great cosmic force, some spectre or demonic entity, something alien and very much not us, that we can band against to fight in a triumph of spirit and survival; the other which is inherently more intimate, human in fact, in which we are the enemy. Classic examples of both would be *The Exorcist*, *Rosemary's Baby* and *The Colour out of Space* against something like *The Face that Must Die* or The *Silence of the Lambs*.

You see the difference?

Now, one of the most obvious reasons for this could well be political. If you look at those strong industrial regions there's a traditional left-wing slant as opposed to the more rural conservative bias, because these areas are all about people and machines, industry being the lifeblood flowing through their veins. There's something almost cosy, and definitively conservative about the horrors of writers like Lovecraft, versus the subversion of something like Ramsey Campbell's *The Face that Must Die* or Clive Barker's *The Body Politic* or *The Inhuman Condition*. Of course, it's all cyclical, as we enter recessions and depressions, the natural desire is to combat a foe we can band together against, a foe to take our minds off austerity, and when we're in times of plenty the natural instinct is to look for the enemy within, the self-sabotaging human weakness, or just plain evil.

So, what is industrial horror?

Is it the smoke stacks and gas towers? Is it the metal cranes of the shipyards turned golem?

The fact is horror is so deeply rooted in who we are, going all the way back to the ancient kingdoms of Sumeria, where they wrote of the vampiric Emikku, or the more supernaturally obsessed works produced post-Inquisition with emphasis on Satan and Witchcraft driving their narratives – from Dante's *Inferno* to *Paradise Lost*, almost three centuries of identical obsessions. It's hardly surprising though, given the Vatican's demands to restore the faith, and weighty tomes with catchy titles like *The Hammer of the Witches* being written before Shakespeare took witches to the London stage, along with ghosts and some seriously gruesome outcomes of which murder was quite the most mundane.

This three hundred year period was all about the

supernatural, but it lead into one of the most enduring forms of horror, the gothic novel, championed by the likes of Anne Radcliffe (*The Mysteries of Udolpho*), Matthew Lewis (*The Monk*), Horace Walpole (*The Castle of Otranto*) that so influenced Polidori, Byron, Shelley, Walter Scott and eventually Poe. What set these aside was the fascination with death and mortality. It wasn't about Satan or witchcraft anymore, it was darker, broody, with the barren landscapes almost becoming characters themselves.

The world doesn't sit still though, and the literature we consume reflects that. The biggest change of all happened around this time, with the advent of the Industrial Revolution (see, there's a point, it all links to industry and industrial horror, I swear) we saw a rise in non-romanticised horrors, no more lurking father-figure's prowling through the dark castle corridors at night, now it was the demon barber of Fleet Street and Stoker's *Dracula*, *Wagner the Werewolf* and *Varney the Vampire*, all of these pulpy stories being churned out in the Penny Dreadfuls. We're moving into the true industrial age, and man's propensity for evil is really coming to the fore. The newspapers are full of horrors like Jack the Ripper, while the writers are fixating on the human monster, be it Stephenson's *Dr Jekyll vs Mr Hyde* or Belloc Lowndes's *The Lodger*, we're steadily moving towards what we'd consider modern horror, where the enemy is very much *us*.

You can see the effects of the Great Depression and

World War II on the literature of subversion, be it Matheson's *I Am Legend* or Jackson's *Haunting of Hill House*, they're very much products of their time and what has been happening in the world around them. How can they not be? But you know what else is starting to happen? The birth of the modern serial killer, with the notorious Ed Gein, which inspired Hitchcock's *Psycho* and Thomas Harris's *The Silence of the Lambs*. The Cold War spawned King and Herbert, and so it goes and so it goes.

So how could the books we grew up on in the 90s and 00s not be intrinsically linked to the industrial roots of their writers? How could the homelessness problem not factor into the writing of Stephen Laws's *Macabre*? How could the riots in Liverpool not filter into Ramsey Campbell's novels about Toxteth? How could the horrors of the corporals killings of 1988 where two British soldiers drove inadvertently into the procession of an IRA funeral not influence Joe Donnelly's *The Shee*? The Miners Strike? Graham Joyce's *The Year of the Ladybird*. The Cleveland Child Abuse scandal? Stephen Gallagher's *Nightmare, with Angel*. And so on. Forget nature, it's all about nurture, and horror, and the stuff of our nightmares has been evolving since the industrial revolution and the rise of the machines...

They aren't our friends. We were told they would bring freedom and leisure time, three day weeks and the like, but what they brought was redundancy, replacement, and the scrap heaps of life. How can you not look for horror in something capable of so much wholesale destruction of hope?

And that's what's waiting for you in here, the wholesale destruction of hope at the hands of twisted industrial landscapes, smoke stacks and gas towers and metal golems that have no souls, no spirits, and can so easily drape themselves in our skins and walk in our shoes, doing everything we can do, faster, and with ruthless efficiency, removing the need for us. That's the world these stories live in, and it's a bleak place. And I can honestly say it's all my fault, because I'm the one who put Dean, our esteemed editor, and Emma, our equally esteemed publisher together and told them to make beautiful books. Yep. It's all my fault.

You can thank me later.

Steven Savile
2nd May 2018
SALA, Sweden

INTRODUCTION

It is always a pleasure (as a compiler / editor) when I ask writers to work with me and when they say yes – as well as being a pleasure, it is an honour. I can never rest on my laurels either as a writer because my colleagues, my *friends*, raise the bar to such an extent that I want...I have to be...better than I have ever been previously.

This time around I have worked with a mixture of the new and the old and by that I mean writers I haven't worked with before or for a while but I'm sure you will agree, everybody is at the top of their game. I hope you enjoy their stories as much as I do.

I am grateful too for Emma / Snowbooks for publishing our work – it is very much appreciated.

I was going to wax lyrical for a few pages about what Industrial Horror means to me or the fact that it can be a very broad church (as is borne out by the stories that follow) but why waste your time when Mr Savile has already done it so eloquently for us – let's just get on with the show, hey? I've worked with Steven a couple of times now and he never lets me down (especially as he is a fellow Spurs supporter) – so thank you Steve – I owe you one.

If you don't mind, I would also like to take this opportunity to thank the following who have been (in their own ways) instrumental in making this book possible:

Jeff Noon; William Gibson; Clive Barker; Ramsey Campbell; David Mitchell; John Fowles; Umberto Eco; Christopher Fowler; Michael Hutchence; Robbie Robertson; Bradley Simpson; John Mellencamp; Tom Waits; Vincent Rottiers; Thomas Doret; Emile Berling; Dominique Frot; Warren Beatty; Paul Kane; Simon Bestwick; Mark West; Terry Grimwood; Mark & Ingrid; Gary; Alfred; Neil; Pam; Anne; Katy; Chris; Niven, Janine, Sarah & Emily; Ed; Suzie; Natalie & Lionel. My mother; Nigel, Zac & Alex; Simon, Charley & George.

To the contributors who trusted me with their work.

And finally to you, Dear Reader, for purchasing *Thread Of The Infinite...*

Enjoy!

Peace and Love.
Dean M. Drinkel
Cannes, France
May 2018

In the City of Concrete Dandelions

By Cate Gardner

Even as the stool legs splintered beneath Mother, she continued instructing Gaia in the way of the stitch. The gag about Gaia's mouth itched. No matter how much she fussed with it, she knew that neither Mother nor Father would allow her to remove the rag they'd wound around her mouth. They wouldn't risk the machines catching the high, childish timbre of her voice. They'd already lost five children to the machines.

Mother jabbed a needle into the back of Gaia's hand. "No daydream. Sew."

Gaia bent her head to her work, the repairing of their neighbours' torn and ragged clothes. Shoulders hunched, they sat before a defunct electric fire on which they'd painted false flames - an illusion of heat in a place where the inhabitants wished life an illusion, a nightmare from which a pinch would wake them. Father sat in his beloved leather chair writing notes in the margins of the newspaper. His anarchy. He coughed into his fist causing the newspaper to scatter across the floor and Mother to pause at her stitching. Father wiped blood from his lips.

To Gaia, fear tasted of phlegm and a sodden rag. Crooked stitches cut across a dirt-rose fabric. If Mother noticed them, Gaia would have to unstitch and start again. As the clock on the mantelpiece chimed midnight, Mother allowed Gaia to put down her work and to climb into the cot in the corner of the room. Mother would sleep on the splintering stool, Father in his chair.

In the dark of the room, the ceiling creaked. The man in the rooms above theirs spent his evenings dancing with the wife he'd lost. Sometimes he giggled to recall the sound of the children that the machines had munched. The sound always made Mother cry. Gaia climbed from the bed, tiptoed across the room, and opened the door into the hallway. Music floated down the stairs. A lullaby. This night she didn't climb the stairs to peer through the crack in the door to the man's apartment. This night she removed her gag and stepped outside.

For several minutes, Gaia remained on the doorstep looking into the night. Then, as if the machines chased her, she raced along their road and the neighbouring street until she came to the park. Wading through grasses and weeds almost as tall as her, Gaia aimed for the rusted remains of the swing park. Laughter echoed from the hollow as small figures brushed by her in their rush to play. The night offered them a few hours to be children. Gaia didn't play on the swings or rush down slides that left legs and hands marked red with rust. Gaia lay on the ground where the grasses were thin and sharp and listened to the earth. Her fist curled around a dandelion. The earth spoke to her. It told her it couldn't breathe. Gaia understood. She couldn't breathe either.

Back home, skin wet from the early morning dew, she crawled under the thin eiderdown just as her parents began to stir. She wrapped her tiny fists around the fabric as Mother began to pull at it.

"Up," Mother said.

As usual, the breakfast porridge was more water than oats. Father settled to read the newspaper he'd read the day before and the day before that - soon, there'd be no space left in the margins for him to write his thoughts. Gaia sat cross-legged before the broken electric fire, sewing together patches of fabric that threatened to disintegrate beneath her oily fingers. When she looked up from her work four or five hours later, she realised Father wasn't in his chair. Again, Mother stuck a pin into Gaia's hand only this time it remained jabbed against bone as if the chair had distracted Mother, she too disturbed by it.

"Work," Mother said, but there was a wistfulness to her voice.

As daylight gave way to darkness, as eyes struggled to stay open, Mother picked up Father's newspaper and studied the words in the margins. Tears pricked her eyes. She crushed the newspaper in her fists, then smoothed it out and reread his words. The following day, a man with shiny shoes and an expensive cloth suit handed Mother a briefcase containing money. Gaia and Mother left the room of the small house, left the street, and headed towards the city that ate children.

Despite that children attended schools in the city and that they didn't spend their days mending rags, Gaia stayed home. This new apartment with its plush furniture, working fire, potted spider plant and plentiful food were as much jail as their old rooms. More so, for she couldn't sneak out at night and converse with her beloved earth. She contented with sitting by the window, with its view of tower blocks of glass and brick, and conversing with the spider plant. It cried for the world too.

At least she no longer had to wear her gag. Not that she talked much. When you've spent most of your life minding your tongue, forbidden to speak, you grow used to thinking rather than saying. She understood Mother's silence; after all, she too had spent her childhood wearing a gag and hidden in a room darker and damper than the house they'd left behind.

The spider plant died on her fourteenth birthday. Mother died three days later. Gaia sat in the bedroom holding Mother's hand until it grew cold and began to stink. When neighbours investigated the smell, discovering Gaia alone, they traced their fingers along her arm and promised to look after her. Their words, their touch, made her want to run.

Coffin-bearers carried Mother from her bed. Gaia followed them from the apartment, the remains of the spider plant and its pot clutched to her chest. The <u>Garden of Rest</u> proved to be a grey building, which despite its title had no actual garden.

She recognised some of the people at the funeral as the neighbours who had discovered her mother's corpse. The sisters who moved in harmony together, tall and graceful, and their smiles revealed a second set of lips, their skin a little loose in places namely chin and under the arms. Beside them, a fearsome man as wide as he was tall, with permanently clenched fists. They seemed to believe themselves her guardians now.

Her skin fascinated them. They said so. They crowded. She flinched from their touch. Both coffin and spider plant disappeared behind a curtain. The black car waited to take her back to the apartment building and, reasons unknown to Gaia, the women and their companion climbed in beside her, shuffling her to the middle.

"You don't mind. You're such a good child."

Gaia gathered all of her fourteen years and with several cracks and hesitations to her voice, she wasn't used to talking to people, she said, "Not a child. Look young."

"How old is not a child?" the women asked.

In a world where machines eat the children of the ghettos, and not knowing if her mother's death meant a return to those terraced streets, she thought of an age far past her own.

"Twenty-four," she said.

Despite the solemn occasion, the women laughed. Gaia shrunk within her skin; bones constricting, folding away from flesh, until she looked wizened, haggard and older than the twenty-four years she claimed. Of all the streets they travelled through, she did not see a single tree or even a leaf blowing on the wind. She would rather hide from the machines in the old grey streets of her childhood.

The sisters accompanied her all the way to her apartment door. In the quiet of the rooms, Gaia wound the old gag around her mouth. The machines may come for unaccompanied children. Shadows lurked outside the apartment door, pacing in tandem. For the next four years, the sisters and their thuggish friend visited but Gaia didn't let them in nor did she allow past the threshold the people who delivered food and plants and compost and fabric, needle and cotton. Sometimes the sisters asked her to sew things for them. *Make us prettier.* She always declined. Gaia remained in self-imprisonment until her eighteenth birthday.

On the dawn of her adulthood, Gaia opened the door to her mother's bedroom. For a moment, she thought the bed still held the imprint of her long-deceased mother but it was merely the disarray of covers and sheets. Despite the passage of time, tears pricked. Searching through her mother's belongings, Gaia discovered a yellowed-newspaper with scribblings in the margins and beneath and around pictures. Memories flooded. Most of the words were illegible but amongst the madness were three sentences of intent.

My darlings, I heard from a man who knows a man that I can save our last and only daughter. I am to be part of the machine and you are to move to the safety of the city. God willing, I will return on the day of our daughter's adulthood.

Carrying the newspaper with her, Gaia climbed onto the windowsill and looked across the city. If Father were still out there, he'd find her. Running her fingers along the ridge of a leaf, she soothed its anguish. They were family too. As the sun blazed orange against the horizon, Gaia unfurled stiff limbs. He wasn't coming.

After three days of waiting for a Father who did not return, she weakened and allowed the sisters into the apartment. This fresh grief left her open to persuasion so when they told her of a place in the heart of the city where trees and flowers grew, she accepted their offer to take her there.

"Don't forget your needles," the sisters said.

I am to be part of the machine and you are to move to the safety of the city.

"Do you know where the machine is?" Gaia asked. "My Father is there."

"Behind the place where the flowers grow."

She trusted neither the sisters nor their companion and yet she'd given them valuable information, facts with which to bribe her. One of the sisters slid around the collection of potted plants.

The sister who remained by the doorway said, "Oh, careful you don't rip your skins, sister."

Gaia wondered if the sisters had names. They must have and yet both seemed reluctant to address themselves as anything other than sister. The plants whispered for Gaia to run. The word *danger* exploded within her ears. These women couldn't feed her to the machines. She'd reached adulthood.

"You will show me garden and machine?"

They nodded, lips parting to reveal an extra layer of skin beneath. What strange creatures they were? In some ways, they seemed delicate - roses with thorns to prick and bleed, yet petals to fall.

Either bravery or stupidity caused her to accompany them, most of it to do with wanting to be in a place where trees grew. They waited by the elevator. She shuddered at the idea of being in such close quarters with them. The sisters and their thuggish friend followed her to the staircase. Outside, the world hummed - the buzz of machines rather than the whisper of grass and leaves, the outstretched limbs of trees. A graffiti artist had drawn giant dandelions on a grey concrete wall. Gaia and the sisters boarded a bus full of people with fixed smiles that offered no laugh-lines. The windows were two-way, which meant passengers could see out but those on the streets couldn't see in - the perfect way for monsters to travel.

Gaia sat in an aisle seat. From the route the bus took, it seemed both machine and garden weren't in the city but on the other side of the streets that she'd grown up in. As the bus wound through familiar territory, Gaia stood up. A sister caught her wrist, but Gaia shook her off. Cold dead grip.

"Stop bus."

The bus continued along the streets as Gaia made her way down the aisle. At the front she repeated, "Stop bus." This time the driver obliged.

Neither sisters nor thug followed her here. In these streets, the bus trundling on without her, Gaia could breathe. Ghost faces peered from behind grime-covered windows, pale faced children. She recalled the ache of looking out at the world. The weeds at the swing park seemed stunted in comparison to their height of childhood. A path wound through the nettles. Of the actual swing park, only skeletons remained. Gaia lay on the earth and listened to its welcoming sighs.

When the moon stretched its light across her prone form, Gaia stood and headed into the streets. Children clung to the dark walls as they made their way to wherever their current meeting place was. In the distance, machines rumbled. A girl of about six or seven stopped to assess Gaia. Did she now look of the city? Before Gaia could speak, before she could reassure, a machine turned the corner. A man of impossible height and who had an extra set of arms, stepped out of the machine and walked towards them. Neither Gaia nor the child ran, the thought was there but the action was not. The man scooped the child up.

Gaia found the strength to move. She kicked at the man, but he brushed her aside, knocking her to the ground. She should be thankful he didn't take her too. The man dropped the child into the back of the machine. Gaia pulled at the door but it wouldn't open. Cold metal beneath desperate hands and a thud from inside as the girl tried to escape. They couldn't do this. The machine rushed away from her leaving only the echo of screams.

Now her steps dragged as she made her way through the streets until she found a familiar door. A different family now lived in the rooms that had been hers but she hoped the music man still danced above. The front door of the house hung open, hanging off broken hinges. Music floated down the stairs. Gaia climbed. She rapped on the music man's door.

"It's Gaia mister. Gaia from downstairs."

Floorboards creaked. When he opened the door, the music man looked thirty years older and a hundred years tired. He didn't recognise her. When last they'd met, she'd been small and afraid, now she was just afraid.

"Like to dance with you," she said.

He welcomed her in. For a brief moment, she played the daughter he'd lost and she offered him both laughter and tears, the former in short supply for them both. A bittersweet interlude. In the end, he remembered the little girl she'd been and thanked her with his final breath. He could return to the earth now. She envied him that.

Back in the city, the earth gagged by concrete and fake grass, the world ceased its whisper and returned to hum. The sisters waited for her. When they boarded the bus this time, they kept her between them and she didn't fight because all she wanted was the trees and her father.

There were no trees. There were only the machines that tore skin from babies and children, only blood and screams and tears.

Large black gates slammed shut behind her as both sisters and their friend pushed her towards the brick building with its imposing chimneys that belched black smoke. They sold Gaia for a fresh suit of baby skin and they slid said suits over their already loose skin. Gaia belonged to the machine now.

The skins of babies and children lay stretched out in refrigeration units, waiting for seamstresses to make breasts and faces for those who should have begun rotting in the earth. For selling her into servitude for the machines, the sisters were entitled to a fresh suit biennially. With each visit, Gaia noted fresh marks in her skin and was thankful for them.

In her break times, and over the space of decades, Gaia searched the cutting lines for her father, but in a place where men spent their days skinning dead children, said men did not last for long. They did this to save their families from this fate. She would not find her actual father here, the man who scribbled in a newspaper, but she would find an approximation of him.

When a baby with skin the colour of the night she'd once played in lay on her table, Gaia put down her needle and sobbed. The skin carried the scent of grasses as if the machines had scooped it from the earth, from where it lay and listened to nature's whispers. She climbed onto the far worktable and peered out at the darkening day. Her window overlooked the yard where the machines unloaded stolen children. As Gaia sobbed, it began to rain. A flood washed everyone from the yard.

As she stretched and worked the skin around a mask of the recipients face, the sky offered thunderclaps and lightning strikes. The roof bulged beneath the weight of the deluge. Sometimes you cannot take anymore and Gaia wondered how she had not reached this point until now. When her mother taught her the stitch, she couldn't have envisioned this.

Moving from her workroom to the break area, she passed men who carried their weariness in their shoulders, knives dripping from desperate, sorrowful fingers. A hurricane shook the windowpanes, rattling glass and wood. The machines had no right to do this, to enslave them. How many days had passed since she entered the machine's employ?

How many lost years?

As another vehicle load of children pulled up at the gates, the factory roof caved in. Despite the gag, despite the long hours sewing until her hands ached, she wished to be home with parents missing or long dead. As glass smashed, Gaia dropped the mask, climbed onto a table and, knocking the glass away, she climbed onto the ledge and out into the yard. The men who had given up their lives for their families followed her trail of blood. Now they used their knives to cut down the fences, freeing first the children and then themselves.

The streets emptied as they paraded through them. Monsters begotten of monsters with the children huddled amongst them. They would head into the city, they would remove the stolen skin, and they would bring it to her.

***

In the house where she'd spent her formative years, Gaia sat before the fire. She stitched. Although her fingers ached with the gnaw of age, she was determined to continue sewing until all of the skin had been returned to and wrapped around bones and organs. The magic in her stitches brought life and blood in bodies that weren't traditionally arranged. In the street outside her little home, and despite the daylight, children laughed and chattered and lived. The old city remained, but the inhabitants now were a rotten few yet to return to ground or air. There were no machines.

With a screech, the latest child borne of her stitch

squirmed in her lap. It warmed its skin before the fire while she fetched it clothes from a burlap sack placed on her father's chair.

"Who am I?" the child asked.

They all found their way in the end once the others welcomed them. Some of the children she'd stitched had reached adulthood now. It had taken longer than she had expected, but the last skin was returned the last bones. Placing the sack on the threadbare carpet, she rested in her father's chair; her eyes too heavy to stay open a moment longer. She dreamt of returning to the earth. Gaia rose on unsteady legs and crossed the terraced streets to the remains of the old swing park.

Come lie with us again, the earth whispered and the children covered her with flowers and soil and she slept forevermore.

A Night In The Bone Factory

By Adrian Cole

Where do I begin with this mess? Probably when Scraggs and me saw that thing in the corridors at Varga Steel, soon after we started there. I would've dismissed it as hallucination, overactive imagination, except for what happened after.

Scraggs was a nervous bugger anyway. Bloody good mechanic, same as me, but he always walked on eggs. In Varga Steel he was crapping himself from the moment we set foot inside the place. But I'll get to that.

That corridor was strictly out of bounds. It was dirty, walls slick with oil, floor puddled and sticky. As Scraggs and I went along it, looking at each other like a couple of kids up to our necks in trouble, we saw a right turn ahead, barely lit by a bulb in the wall, smothered in web, speckled with dead flies.

Something slid out along the floor from the turning, like it had been pushed into the corridor. It looked like a twisted spar of metal, its front end divided into several thin rods. Getting closer, we realised it wasn't.

It was a human arm. Severed at the elbow - there were ligaments and shreds of flesh – or so we thought – dangling from the cut end. I say cut, but as we gaped at it, it looked more like it had been yanked free of its body, like a chicken leg torn from a carcass. There wasn't a lot of blood, but it was leaking, the fluids thick and coagulating. And the smell was foul, like meat that's been gone off for days.

It moved. That was the real pisser. It fucking *moved*. I know limbs and even heads can still twitch after they've been separated. This wasn't twitching, though. The hand was clenching and unclenching, fingers wriggling, like the arm was still part of a functioning body. Worse, the thing slid forward, a rigid snake, fingers scratching for hold in the oily pools. Like it was searching for something.

Scraggs was pissing himself, so terrified he couldn't speak. I just swore. We needed to get the fuck out of there. We swung round - our supervisor was looking at us. His eyes were half shut, his stare cold and nasty. More like snake's eyes than a human's. He sure as hell didn't want us seeing what we had just seen.

"You in wrong place," he said.

He fucking got that right.

***

A few days before, I was in the *Boilermaker's Arms* with Scraggs and three other mates, drowning our sorrows, empty pint glasses piling up. All five of us had been made redundant, the small factory where we worked closed down. The owner had died and his son wasn't interested in taking the business on, so he'd sold it to a developer. The factory would be bulldozed to make way for a block of offices. To line the pockets of someone who already stank of money.

A whole lot of us were just dumped on the scrapheap, unless we could find something else. All in our mid-twenties, looking ahead to a lifetime in employment. In this city, twenty years ago, when I was still kicking a ball round the playground, there were enough jobs for everyone. My dad had never been out of work. Not that it did him much good in the end. Asbestosis finished him while I was still learning my trade.

Different now. Finding a job, especially when hundreds of you got thrown out, was a bastard. For me and Scraggs it was bad enough, but for Mick, Aggie and Stan it was far worse - they all had wives and young kids - dropping on to the dole was a real bummer. You could see the desperation in their eyes, even when they tried to laugh it off through the beer. Apart from losing a good wage, there was the nightmare of not working. All of us liked what we did. We moaned about it, like everyone else, but it was good to work. We were all skilled tradesmen.

Mick said, "I know a small garage. Sometimes they get more work than they can handle. They'll give me something – casual stuff."

"I thought about starting up on me own," said Aggie, but without conviction. We all knew he was the least organized of us. Normally we'd have taken the piss, but we just nodded. We needed encouragement, something to hang on to.

Scraggs stared into his beer glass, swirling its dregs. "There's always Varga Steel. Last resort."

It was like someone had dumped something dirty on the table.

"Last resort is fucking right," said Stan, who always said least. Not that he didn't enjoy being part of our group; he was just not a big talker. We could see he was rattled by Scraggs' suggestion.

"You know anything about Varga Steel – apart from its reputation?" I asked him.

"Had a mate who worked there for six months. He was as tight-lipped about the place. He was never the same when he came out. Like he'd been to hell and back. I don't know what the fuck they do in that place, but it leaves a mark."

"Where's your mate now?" said Scraggs.

"Last I heard, in hospital. Nervous breakdown. Got into pill popping, big time. He was clean – never as much as sniffed a pill – until he came out of Varga Steel."

Mick and Aggie were both nodding, hands tightening around their pints. "I've heard stories like that," said Mick. "They never take anyone on long term. Pay is supposed to be very good. But whatever you do for them, it fucks you up. Me, I'd rather be on the dole than go there."

Aggie growled agreement.

"What the fuck *do* they do?" said Scraggs. "Engineering, that right? Vehicles and the like."

"Specialise in big trucks, freight," said Stan. "And wreck recovery. The really big stuff. I heard they deal with any kind of wreckage – trains, aircraft. You name it."

"Salvage?" I said.

Stan shrugged. "Only one way to find out, if any of you guys have got the balls."

Mick and Aggie sat back, murmuring their disinterest. Until now, none of us would have contemplated working at Varga Steel. And obviously, desperate or not, these guys were not up for it. Anywhere else. Road sweeping, stacking shelves, they'd do that.

I looked at Scraggs and he knew that look. We'd been mates since primary school, glued together like a couple of Siamese twins. When we were still young – and stupid – enough, we'd played all the dare games you can think of, including the reckless 'chicken'. Railway lines. In our street, the railway ran along the back of our cramped gardens. We used to challenge other groups of kids to see who'd be last to get off the track when a diesel came down the line. Me and Scraggs were the best at it. Got cocky with it and bloody nearly got killed more than once. Yeah, if there was a dare going, no matter how fucking stupid, we'd take it on. Earned a lot of respect. We were idiots.

Scraggs had always been terrified, but he wanted to impress me, his big mate. I knew it later, realised how bloody selfish I'd been making the poor bastard take all that crap just so he could keep up with me. Some fucking mate I was.

Scraggs put down the empty glass. "Was a time," he said, "when no one challenged me and you, Dom, without us taking them on."

"We're not gormless kids anymore," I said.

"We're fucking broke, mate. Broke without much hope."

Aggie was scowling, his hands actually shaking. "You mad fuckers aren't seriously thinking about working for Varga Steel?"

"They take on short term," I said. "We could do six months, until something better comes along. How do you get in?"

"There's a guy they call the Caucasian," said Stan. "A Russian or something. He does the recruiting. Down at the *Old Crown*. Can't miss the fucker. He's the size of a house. If you guys are serious, good luck to you. But you have to be crazy to do this."

"Yeah," said Mick. He put his hand on Scraggs' arm.

"Scraggsie, son, leave this one out. Really. You don't want to go there."

Scraggs looked at me, and something was stirring in his expression. Maybe it was the ghost of the wild kid I'd known. His turn to put *me* on the spot. "Can't do any harm to check it out."

I couldn't argue.

***

It was easy enough to find the big Caucasian. He was a dead ringer for that heavyweight boxer, the world champ. Must've been seven foot tall and half as wide. The *Old Crown* was a dump, a wreck of a place that prided itself on being part of the past, a kind of grime shrine to the original concept of the working classes. The only thing missing was the cigarette smoke, but I doubt if anyone would've raised an eyebrow if the crowd in there had started lighting up.

The Caucasian stared at me and Scraggs, his face like stone. Looked like it had never known a smile, or any expression. He listened to me as I asked him about getting work at Varga Steel.

"Mechanics?" he said, mangling the word so I barely recognised it. "Sure. Varga want mechanics. You good, huh? Very good?"

"The best."

"We give you try out, huh? Start Monday." He told us where to go. Scraggs and me knew the place. We had another day to think about it.

***

I thought Scraggsie might change his mind, but come the day, he picked me up in his beat-up old Zephyr and we drove through a part of the city that was either falling into ruin, due for redevelopment, or had been turned into huge mounds of brick and rubble. I was surprised at how extensive this rotten part of the inner zone was, like a giant bone-yard, an industrial cemetery. Depressing to think once it would have been thriving – filthy and smoke-clogged, yeah, but like a big pumping heart of industry. We passed a couple of canals that hadn't been reclaimed yet, their water more like oil, choked with junk.

There were usually a bunch of homeless people in these run-down streets, cooped up under grimy railway arches, buried under old papers, nicked shopping trolleys nearby. But apart from one or two deadbeats, there was no one around. The whole area was abandoned, like it had been bombed in the War and just left.

Varga Steel was part of a complex of old warehouses and factories, almost buried under the ruins around it, so you'd never have thought anything was done in there. There was a modern steel fence around the place, riddled with very nasty razor wire. I'd heard anyone caught breaking in had a real tough time of it. We found the gates and two guards in uniform met us. Big guys with granite faces, minor versions of the Caucasian. There was a steel hut to one side and I swear they had guns in there, like this was a border check point. It reminded me of films I'd seen about the Iron Curtain.

We mentioned the Caucasian and they let us in. The factory was big, like those once thriving huge car factories of this city, all gone now. The building swallowed us and I could feel Scraggs' unease already. He looked like he'd turn and make a bolt for it at any moment. I wasn't feeling so hot about this myself. But we needed work.

They gave us plenty to do for starters. Simple stuff, working mainly with metal, part of their reclamation programme, selecting the least damaged parts of machines that had been involved in industrial accidents and making them serviceable. We were good at this sort of thing, although we weren't always sure what it was we were fixing. Some of that equipment was odd, impossible to define. If it was from vehicles or other machines, we couldn't always tell.

We were warned not to stray from where we worked, just stick to what we were given. So we didn't get to see what happened to the stuff we worked on. It was a component part of something else, something newer, but no one said anything about it. A few other guys worked with us, but they were like dummies - hardly spoke. Looked like they'd been on piecework for years, worn down by the monotony, eyes dull, brains duller.

"I can just about manage six months of this," Scraggs said. "But I ain't gonna end up like these bastards. Fucking robots."

He was right. We were skilled men and we liked a challenge. Whoever was checking our work must have thought so, too. After a week of the drudgery, we were taken to another area. It was more sophisticated. There was construction going on, more intricate steel work.

Our supervisor was another mid-European. He used few words. Basically he showed us what he wanted. He pointed out a steel door at the one side of the factory floor. It was scarred with a big symbol, nothing I recognised. A no go area. If we went there, we'd pay for it, probably in broken bones. This place was run like an army base. Very tough discipline. No one argued. I guess it meant sleek productivity.

Scraggs and me were the only Brits in the small group that worked on our components - probably deliberate management policy. None of the guys near us could speak more than two or three words of English, so there was no communication, no chit-chat. They could make themselves understood as far as the work went, using basic sign language and demonstration. No tea breaks, no radios. The days dragged. At least there were no complaints about our work.

I daresay we would have stuck it out for the whole mind-numbing six months if things had gone on in that laborious, automated way. But there was an incident that slung a real spanner in the works.

Scraggs and me were carrying a piece of kit we'd put together, under instruction, to another part of the factory. A section of engine, maybe for a big generator. We delivered it to another bunch of guys and helped attach it to whatever they'd been working on. It went on a wide metal table, its legs reinforced so it could stand heavy loads. Resting on it was a weird-looking mass of interlocking steel, a lot of tubes and rods sticking out of it. Christ knows what it was.

Me and Scraggs offered up our section and three guys began using their spanners to integrate it. While they were doing it, the main body of the machine started to vibrate, like an engine inside it had been switched on. I guess it wasn't meant to happen, because the other guys all jumped back, like they'd had their hands burned. That machine – it revved up, smoke drifting from its core, like something had shorted in there.

Then the weirdest fucking thing happened. Those rods and tubes all jerked into life, springing wide open, jointed at the middle and clamping down on to the top of the wide table. It was like a fucking great metal spider. A twisted, incomplete, bastard version, but some kind of spider-thing. It dropped its underbelly, using its legs to spring up, clearing the side of the table awkwardly. It dropped to the floor, more smoke coming out of it.

One guy was holding a spanner the size of a pickaxe. He rushed in at the spider-thing and smashed the spanner down on one of the tube legs. It shattered, the metal splitting. Twice more the guy dealt the thing blows, buckling metal, partially crippling the spider-thing. One of the broken limbs, its end now a jagged point, shot forward and drove into the man's gut. He screamed, wriggling like a maggot on a fish hook, dropping the spanner. Blood sprayed the floor – blood and something else, like it was mixed with a darker, oilier fluid.

Two other men attacked the spider-thing, but they were driven back as it retaliated, swinging more dangerous limbs at them. The gutted man dragged himself off the spit, ripping a flap of his flesh loose - he lurched away, abdomen and legs glistening. Scraggs and me automatically went after him, thinking we'd help, but he moved surprisingly quickly. We followed him back through tall banks of machinery towards our original workplace. There was a hell of a lot of blood and mess coming out of him - it was amazing he could still move.

We caught up with him as he reached for the door we weren't supposed to use. The one with the weird symbol on it. I reached out to drag him back, but he swung his arm at mine and I felt like he'd hit me with the big spanner he'd dropped. Then he had the steel door open, leaning on it, vomiting blood, and went through. The door clanged shut behind him.

The other guys must have subdued the spider-thing - they were here now. But as soon as they saw the wounded man disappear through the door, they turned away, like nothing had happened. They went back to their work.

Scraggs gaped after them. "What the fuck was all that about?" he said.

I looked at the blood on the floor, the pool of vomit. It was mostly blood, though there was oil mixed in with it and the bile. The guy couldn't possibly survive a wound like that. He'd made for this door deliberately, like it was his one hope of getting help.

We went back to the place where the machine had burst into life. The workers there had got rid of it and replaced it with something else, a similar mass of electrical and mechanical bits and pieces that looked like they needed wiring into a bigger product. What blood and muck had been spilled on the floor was gone, mopped up and sterilized.

Scraggs and me knew better than to talk to anyone about the incident, still shaken up by the time we signed off for the day.

Later, in the pub, we agreed not to mention it to our mates. We were marked, left to sit on our own, even when the place got crowded.

A guy in a thick jacket, not a regular, asked if he could sit with us. He'd bought a pint, but he set it down and didn't touch it.

"You guys started at Varga?" he said, leaning forward. The pub's din muffled his words. He had a slightly posh voice. Not from our parts.

"What of it?" I said.

"Good pay?"

"Yeah."

"You could earn a lot more."

"Look, mate," I said, a bit of edge in my voice, "we're not into anything crooked. We don't do drugs and tarts and all that shit. We're mechanics. That's all." I knew there were plenty of dirty rackets on the go, but there was no way I'd ever get mixed up with them, good money or not.

"That's not what I'm looking for. I want a couple of pairs of eyes. Inside Varga."

"Yeah? So who are you?"

"Varga is a bent organization. We know that. You work there long enough, you'll find that out. Come outside and I'll give you all the information you need." He got up casually. "I'll give you five minutes. After that, I'll be gone and we'll forget it. But I'll make it well worth your while."

After he'd gone, I asked Scraggs, "What you reckon?"

"Rival firm?" Scraggs never liked to flinch from a dare, but I could see he was uneasy. I was going to say, forget it, but he got up. "Okay. Let's see what this is about."

Outside, in the car park, there was a street light near the wall at its end. There was a big black van parked there and the guy who'd spoken to us was leaning on it, smoking. The back of the van was open and there was a load of equipment in there, like TV tracking stuff, with another guy crouched over it, fat earphones wrapped round his head.

"Get in," said the guy. "We need to drive somewhere more quiet."

No way was I going to do that, but when I turned to tell him to fuck off, I was looking down at a gun. I'd never seen one other than on the telly, or in a movie before. And there was another guy nearby. Maybe he had a gun, too.

Scraggs swore, but the guy smiled. "Just a precaution. Get in."

We clambered aboard and slid on to the seats. The guy sat opposite, his mate closing the doors. I heard him get in the front. In a moment we drove away.

"I'm Cray." The man slipped his gun inside his jacket. "I work for the Government. You're under my protection."

"You hold a fucking gun on us," said Scraggs, "and you're protecting us? The fuck."

Cray's face was a weird colour in the glow of the instruments. It made him look older than what he was – I reckon about forty. "Tell me about Varga Steel," he said calmly.

He coaxed out of us what we'd seen, the freakish spider-thing and the guy who'd been near enough gutted. Cray never flinched, like he'd been expecting something like this.

"If you're trying to nail Varga for illegal activities," said

Scraggs, "how come you don't raid them? Close them down?"

The van had stopped, probably in the middle of nowhere. "It's well organized," said Cray. "Their industrial skills are very high tech. State of the art. There's an area in there they can seal so tightly it would be impossible to find. We've tried it – and failed. We won't be allowed to do it again. We need a more subtle approach."

"A couple of mugs like us," I said.

"Trojan horse, guys. You go in and unlock the secret door for us. We'll pay you a whole lot more than they will."

Scraggs swore. "When they find out who's screwed them, they'll be looking for us."

"No. When we nail them, we take the whole show down for good. You guys won't be given a second thought, I promise you."

***

So that's how we got into this mess. We figured if we refused, Cray would make life even worse for us, like seeing to it we never got work again. But he was offering us a shit-load of money. For another dare. Only way more chilling than the railway tracks.

Back at Varga Steel, we watched the taboo door. Funny it was never locked. Men came and went, sometimes workers, sometimes management. Some carried tools, others clipboards. Never any guards. Being told to keep out was enough for the workforce. We all worked in silence, apart from a few instructions, like a bunch of machines, everyone focused on the work. No banter, no singing, no camaraderie. Fucking weird.

After three days, ending a long shift, in the early evening, me and Scraggs were among the last to leave. It was our best chance of checking out the forbidden zone. So after a last look around we headed slowly for that door. We got to within a few feet of it, when the fucking thing opened. Our supervisor came out. He must have known immediately what we were up to. His expression didn't change. Same old frozen look, face blank.

He pointed at us. "You men do good work," he said. "We give you better now. We lost a man. You replace." His words caught us cold, like a slap.

I nodded. Scraggs just stood still - I could feel him shaking.

The supervisor held open the steel door. "Come. I show you work. You stay late. More money, yes?"

We followed the guy into the shadows beyond the door. It swung shut behind us without a sound. The supervisor led us down a long corridor, its walls bare, empty metal, like it was a big air duct. Half way down it was a stairwell - we followed the supervisor down several landings. We must have been well underground. Below was a wider room, with a few annexes off it. I heard voices, low and garbled, so I couldn't catch the words.

There seemed to be a lot of people in the shadows.

Our supervisor gestured impatiently for us to follow, ignoring whoever was there. I heard what sounded like chains rattling, dragging over the steel floor. A couple of shapes edged out of darkness and me and Scraggs both jumped. These men were filthy, clothed in rags, their faces and hands dark with grime, like they'd been working in an open cast mine. It took me a moment to understand who they were. Homeless people. We'd noticed there were hardly any in the rundown streets around Varga Steel.

What the fuck were they doing here? Sheltering? I would have believed it, but I saw chains ending in manacles about the wrists of a couple of these shambling wrecks. The faces weren't clear, but desperation in their eyes made me shudder. Something was badly wrong here.

There was no time to check it out – the supervisor led us into another corridor and opened a door into a big store. There were loads of racks, packed with lengths of steel, rods and reels of wiring. Suits of armour were hung up. They looked like soldiers - it was too dark to see properly. I thought I saw military uniforms. Other things poked out of crates. Lengths of bone – arm or leg bone, unless I was freaking out.

When we entered another room, a kind of laboratory, I realised I'd been right. There was a full human skeleton hanging up. On the walls were loads of very detailed diagrams of the human form – its bones, muscles, ligaments - the full set.

The lab's centrepiece was a tank, filled with bright blue fluid. As I studied it, the supervisor pressed something underneath it. Inside the tank a slab rose. On it, dripping and steaming, was a human corpse, or a very good model. Electrical wires were connected to its eye sockets and a white tube ran from its nostrils down into the fluid. I could see that parts of the body were metal, not flesh. One steel arm was open. Shit, the whole arm was *a gun*.

"Tomorrow, we show you new work," said the supervisor. He indicated the thing in the tank. "Specialised. Tonight, you sleep there." He pointed to another door.

Scraggs wanted to protest, but I nudged him to silence. I had a feeling we were prisoners here. The supervisor left, closing the main door behind him. We were sure he'd locked us in. Scraggs swore crudely, his face ashen.

"Let's get the fuck out of here," I said. "Has to be a way. These bastards don't intend to let us go, not after seeing all this shit. What the fuck are they doing with all those people up there?"

"Dunno."

We checked out the sleeping quarters – a couple of beds, a toilet and a shower. Small kitchen area, stocked with food for a few days. Until they'd done with us.

All the other doors fed a maze, leading back to our room. Only one locked door. A way out? I found a length of steel that served as a makeshift crowbar and tried prizing the door open.

Took us an hour to wrench the door off its hinges. Another steel corridor beckoned.

We hadn't gone far, when we saw that crawling arm. An experiment gone wrong. Our supervisor had tracked us, now full of menace. I swung up my makeshift crowbar and the man growled deep in his throat, opening his mouth in a snarl. His teeth weren't real. They gleamed, steel, sharp as packed knives. I swung the rod and brought it down across the side of his face. Bone cracked and something fizzed. I'd drawn blood. It sprang from a long cut.

The man staggered, dropping to one knee, and I drove the crowbar into his mouth, ringing on those teeth. Sparks flew from the impact and he collapsed, both his arms clawing at the air in spasm. Blood foamed through his teeth and something leaked from his ears. Scraggs was shouting, obviously fucking terrified. I couldn't blame him – he must have thought I'd gone mad. I knew I had to act, though, or we were finished.

We ran out of there, down another slippery corridor, barely able to see. There were more corridors and weird sights – some parts of this madhouse were like an abattoir, with human carcasses hung up, wired and fused in some kind of lunatic experiment. Beyond a last pair of wider doors we came out into what looked at first like a huge underground parking lot. There were all kinds of vehicles here, but when we found a switch that lit the place up we realised it was a scrapyard. Hundreds of wrecks, mostly cars, had been piled up, some of them ripped open as if they'd been cannibalised for parts. Big trucks, steam engines, row upon row of them; some so old they were rusted all to hell.

Somewhere at the very back of this metal graveyard, there was a wide door, at the top of a ramp. I pointed at it. "That's it, mate. The way out."

"You won't rip that open. It's too big. They'll find us before we have a chance. We must be on CCTV. They'll be here soon, I'll bet."

"Then we'll bust our way out with one of these fuckers." I pointed to the mangled vehicles. "Look for something that we can patch up. Come on, you bastard, we have to try."

So that's what we did. And we got lucky. There was a cleared space among the piles of debris and three cars that had already been worked on. They were no more than chassis, but they had engines and seats. Just missing the finished shell. We didn't need that. We just wanted something we could drive.

Scraggs knew more about car engines than me, so he tinkered about with one of the vehicles while I watched out for any sign of pursuit. None so far.

"Okay, get in!" he called and we leapt up into the seats. As I did so, still clutching the crowbar, I realised that the car's superstructure wasn't made of steel. It was more like – *bone*. It was like we'd got into a big skeleton, twisted and shaped to blend with the machinery. What the fuck was going on in this place?

Scraggs gunned the engine and ground the gears. We took off and he wrenched the vehicle around and headed for the ramp. We braced ourselves as he aimed the snub nose at the door - we hit it full on, ducking down, metal shrieking and buckling. For a moment we were jammed, the engine screeching, but Scraggs coaxed more out of it and we burst through into the cold night air. There were no lights and nothing to guide us and we careered off down a street, bouncing off its walls, showered in sparks.

We were in a deserted part of the city - no night prowlers to dodge. Just as well, given that the car was swinging from side to side, like it had a life of its own. I was about to shout above the din of the engine, when I realised something was wrong. Scraggs was shaking, his whole body rigid, bounced up and down by the wild movement of the vehicle – like a live thing, trying to throw him off.

Something in its structure, an extension of the bone components, twisted and writhed, snapping over his hands, and another shadow merged with his neck, pinning his head. He screamed. The car was *absorbing* him. He was no longer independent of it – he was merging with it, fused to it, his blood flowing into it, its fluids flowing back into him. His face was drawn into a horrific mask, eyes distended, teeth – long, sharp rows of gleaming metal – protruded like some kind of killer predator zooming in on a kill.

I knew if I didn't stop him, he'd lose control of the vehicle, or shoot it into eventual traffic. There was only one thing I could do. I rammed the crowbar into the side of his head. It tore through flesh and bone and clanged up into something more solid, the metamorphosing metal. His head snapped sideways, a component wrenched from a socket. Blood spattered the console and a great rope of thick fluid hung from his mouth. I got a last fleeting look of the friend I had known most of my life, a last despairing expression of horror in his eyes, and then the car hit something, rising and corkscrewing like a bullet and smashed upside down on the tarmac.

I felt ripping, tearing agony in my right arm and then I was clubbed and battered, flung into oblivion.

I must have been unconscious for several minutes. When I came to, I was slumped up against a wall, my lower body sprawled across the pavement. Twenty feet away, the wrecked car was shuddering and contorting, like a giant, maimed spider, trying to right itself, its limbs all busted and fucked. Black smoke poured out of it. It smelled like burned meat. There was no sign of Scraggs and I knew then he was part of that smashed ruin.

As I watched it, unable to move, pinned down by the agonising, throbbing pain down my right side, I saw something struggle out of the debris. It groped its way free of it, a long, bony limb, an arm, whose metallic hand squeezed and un-squeezed, trying to grip the life that was leaking out of it. My own right arm had been sliced off in the crash, mangled and shredded.

***

I must have blacked out again. When I came to, I was here in the hospital. Buried in pillows and a soft mattress. Sheets up to my chin. Drips on either side of me. A nurse nearby, writing something on a clipboard.

"How are you, Mr Thorn? You've had a rough time. You'll be okay."

Rough time? Christ. Too fucking true. My whole body was numb.

Someone moved into my line of sight. It was Cray, in his thick jacket. I wondered if the gun was still tucked inside.

"You did well," he said, leaning over me. The nurse withdrew.

I couldn't move, or speak. I didn't need to ask about Scraggs. I knew the worst.

"So – what have you brought me?" said Cray, almost casually.

And he pulled back the sheets.

Slippery When Wet

By Marie O'Regan

She couldn't have seen what she thought she'd seen. It was impossible.

She rubbed her eyes, forcing her knuckles deep into the sockets until her entire head pulsed with pain, and looked again.

It was still there. The figure stood at the foot of her bed, barely distinguishable in the darkness – but it couldn't hide its size. It was tall, maybe seven feet, perhaps even a little more. In the dim glow afforded by the moonlight it glistened as if wet, the skin itself seemingly mottled, bumpy even. Its throat appeared to pulse as it sucked breath in and then rattled it out. *Like a frog*, she thought. *It's got skin like a frog.*

It sighed, the sound wet and rasping in its deformed throat – and Sarah realised she didn't know if she was looking at something that had even started out as a person. It looked sort of the right shape, that was true, but the details were... off, somehow. As she watched, its colour shifted from greenish black to black with red glints firing up and down its body, and she realised her eyes had now adjusted to the gloom. She wasn't sure that was a good thing. Was it angry?

It was tall, she could see that much, but its arms and legs weren't visible in the darkness, and she found it hard to discern how...wide it was, either. It seemed to be shifting, somehow: one minute thin, the next...not fat, exactly, but more solid. More *there*.

It let out a cry, its voice full of sorrow, and then it was gone.

Sarah realised suddenly that she'd been holding her breath, so let it out in a long, shaky sigh that wasn't far off becoming a sob. It had felt like they stared at each other for ages, but it couldn't have been more than a few seconds. Belatedly, she realised she was terrified, and wondered why she hadn't screamed, why she hadn't thought to pick up her mobile and ring for help, why she hadn't woken Mike. Some damsel in distress she was; couldn't even raise a sound to save herself. She'd just sat there, staring, like an idiot. Fight or flight, my arse. She apparently turned into a vegetable when scared.

What was it? And what did it want with her?

Because it did want something from her; she knew that without a shadow of a doubt. This was the first time she'd actually caught sight of it, that was true, but for weeks now there'd been hints of something out of the ordinary, hadn't there? Strange smells in the hallways, and there was a sickly sweet smell in the bathroom that just wouldn't shift, no matter how much she cleaned it and opened the windows to air it out. She'd even called a plumber, but he'd charged her a fortune just to tell her he couldn't find anything wrong. Mike had just sighed at the bill, angry that she'd cost them money because of what he insisted was hormones.

"It's the baby," he'd said. "Ignore it; it'll settle down once the sickness stops. We can hardly call the police because your sense of smell is off."

And it had, mostly, that was true. But tonight the house smelt as if it belonged at the bottom of a swamp. Her stomach rolled and she groaned, breathing slowly in and out as she prayed it would settle. She didn't want to add the smell of vomit to the foetid odour she was already fighting against.

Shaken, she wondered why her husband hadn't woken up. He'd always been a deep sleeper, she knew, but couldn't he just once wake up when something weird was going on? He'd developed a habit of watching her lately, she knew; he thought she was mad. That angered her, and she decided enough was enough – time he realised she was telling the truth.

"Mike!"

Nothing. She reached out in the dark, ready to shake him into consciousness; punch him awake if necessary – annoyed all over again by how deeply he could sleep. There could be an earthquake and he'd still be snoring.

Except he wasn't. Snoring. Her hand landed on a damp, rumpled patch of sheet and she withdrew it quickly with a grimace, sniffing at it; her face already crumpled in disgust at what she thought she'd find. The moisture on her fingers felt vaguely slimy.

It was just sweat, thank God. She wiped her hand on the covers, making a mental note to change the bed in the morning; that and bleach whatever was in the bathroom out of existence once and for all. A wet bed was not something she wanted to deal with; although she supposed she'd be tackling her fair share in the not too distant future. This was different, though. This was gross.

She called him again, and now even she could hear the quaver in her voice. "Mike?"

Louder now, questioning; worried about her husband for the first time. Then she heard the sound of the toilet flushing and relaxed, waited for him to amble back into the bedroom. The skin on the back of her neck was still crawling; part of her knew she wouldn't relax properly until Mike had searched the house – no matter how much he protested it was all in her head.

He wandered in, a befuddled expression on his face that changed to a smile when he saw she was awake. "Alright?"

"Not really. Someone was standing at the bottom of the bed."

He blinked. Turned the light on and stared at the offending spot of carpet as if it held the answer. "Are you sure?"

"*Of course* I'm sure!"

"Well, where did they go?" He blinked again, owlish with sleep, and rubbed his hand across his eyes.

Sarah hugged the duvet higher around her before she answered. "I was hoping you'd go and look?"

He glared at her, furious. "Why me?"

"Well for a start because you're up..."

"And?"

"And you're bigger than me!" she hissed. "And I'm pregnant!"

"Makes me more of a target," he huffed. "Besides, you were probably just dreaming again. It's not the first time you've woken up thinking something you've dreamed was real and made me go and see, is it?"

She just stared at him. He tried to maintain his sulk for a minute or so, but the sheer dickishness of what he'd just said was sinking in, she could see it happening. So what if it had been a dream? He was supposed to want to make her feel better. A faint flush appeared at his throat, and he dropped his gaze to the floor.

"Some gentleman you are," she muttered, and lay back down, pulling the duvet up and over her head. She could still hear his muttered "Fuck off," though.

The door slammed and he was gone; off to find whatever

or whoever – some kind of animal? – had intruded on their home, however reluctantly.

She couldn't just lie there; she kept thinking she could hear sounds coming from either their bathroom or the stairs. Each time she sat up, of course, there was nothing. "My hero," she muttered as she finally threw off the duvet and got out of bed. Sarah padded to the door and eased it open, held it slightly ajar and placed her ear to the gap. She couldn't hear anything; the house was quiet apart from the sounds Mike made as he blundered through the downstairs of their home. She'd know those anywhere.

Silence fell. Sarah tensed, even held her breath again as if that would mask the sound of someone (or something) approaching. The tension inside built until she thought she'd scream and then he was there. Mike. Standing in front of her as if she was insane, waiting for her to open the door wider so he could get back into the bedroom.

"What?"

He was frowning, fed up with everything. She knew that look of old.

"Where the bloody hell did you come from?" she hissed, and stepped back so that the door could open. She didn't know why she hadn't opened it herself – just that something had made her not want to touch it. Not while he was standing there.

He pushed the door, remaining in the shadowy hall while it swung wide – seemingly unwilling to step into the brightness of the bedroom.

"What's the matter?" she asked, and took another step back.

"It's a bit bright," he snapped. "I've been fumbling around in the dark and you've got it so bright in here we could warn ships."

"It's not that bright, don't be daft."

He stood taller, then, and she wondered how he'd managed to make his shadow move like that against the door. She thought about making a joke about Peter Pan but then the smile trying to reach her lips died, and she focussed – properly focussed – on what was wrong with it.

It was...wavering. Only a little, and it seemed to stop whenever she looked directly at it, but still. It was moving, if only slightly – like jelly wobbling on a plate, just before it settled.

"Mike, what...?"

"Turn the light off."

"What?"

"Turn it off!" he shouted. "It's hurting my eyes."

She stared. He was sweating, the sheen of it making him look sick, feverish. His eyes were watery and did indeed look as if they were burned. "Are you sick again?" she whispered.

He shook his head. "No. Not like that."

"You sure?" She thought back to the hospital visits, the never-ending dependence on what the next blood test would say, and wanted to cry – the thought of going back to that...

"No!" he shouted. "I'm fine."

"Are you taking your meds?"

He smiled at her, and she barely knew him. "Of course I am. They're keeping me alive, after all."

And there it was. The stark fact that underlaid their daily lives – no more worries about his liver, thank God; a nice new one, one of the first grown using stem cell technology. Now they just had to worry about rejection, decay; waiting for the day their nice new life was ripped out from under them and they were back on the waiting list for another transplant – if they got that lucky.

She stared at him, looking for signs of fever, of jaundice… any one of the hundred and one things that lurked at the back of her mind every day like a rabid dog waiting to bite.

He sighed, and moved into the bedroom, careful to hit the light switch first – thankfully only dimming it rather than extinguishing it entirely. He scratched a forearm absently as he sat down, and Sarah found herself staring. He shook his head. "For Christ's sake, Sarah, it's just an itch. It's not everywhere, it's not driving me crazy, there's no rash…it's just because I'm sweating, that's all."

"But why?" she said. "Why are you sweating so much? It's not hot."

He hesitated, and when his answer came she found herself unconvinced. "Just nerves, I guess. I was blundering around in the dark, knocking myself on furniture then rushed back up here to you. I wanted to put your mind at rest. So I'm sweating, okay?"

No. It wasn't. But he wasn't going to give her any more answers now, and whatever she'd seen was gone.

He must have noticed her wavering because he pushed the duvet back and climbed in, gesturing for her to follow. "So can we go back to sleep now? Please? And turn the light off, for God's sake."

She did as he asked, switching off the light completely and climbing into bed only to lie rigid beside her husband as he quickly fell asleep and started to snore.

The house was quiet; that was something, at least. His breathing was not. He'd always snored, but now he was louder than she'd ever heard him; great heaving breaths in and equally huge wheezing breaths out. She was surprised his body could stand the strain.

Finally, she turned on her side and faced him as he slept. He was struggling, and she wondered if this was something else she now had to worry about. Had the snoring finally progressed to sleep apnoea, and all the risks *that* entailed? His throat fluttered, and she gasped. There was no other word for it; the flesh around the side of his neck nearest to her had...fluttered, as if something had moved there as the air rattled in his throat. She leaned closer and watched, holding her breath.

There it was again. The skin itself moved, as if there was some kind of...flap? Realisation dawned and she half-reached out, then pulled her hand back, aghast. Gills? What the...?

Belatedly she realised the snoring had stopped, and she slowly raised her eyes to look Mike in the eye. He was staring right at her, and then he blinked and she screamed. His eyelids had blinked left to right, not down as usual.

The light snapped on, and Mike was standing by the bed now, one hand still on the switch of the bedside lamp. "What the fuck are you screaming at this time?"

She couldn't answer. She just pointed, hand shaking, at his neck.

"What, what is it? Spider?" He was frantic, brushing at his neck in that hectic, disgusted way people bat at insects or arachnids that have dared to touch their skin. Then he touched his neck and stopped, hung his head. "So now you know."

Sarah was backed all the way across the bedroom, back against the closed door. "What do I know, Mike? Tell me what you think I know!" She was trying to keep her voice calm, but failing miserably. She was one step off hysteria, and he knew it.

He was moving, slowly but surely edging around the bed towards her. "It's not what you think."

Sarah laughed. "It can't be!"

His smile was rueful, almost playful, but still he was edging towards her. He was almost within reach. "Well then, maybe it is."

She shook her head, fumbling behind her for the door handle.

"I'm better though, right?" he said, and now he'd stopped, now he was just standing there, hands splayed out towards her in a peace-keeping gesture. *Don't be scared. It's just me.* Except it wasn't just him. Not anymore. "Look at me," he said, and she did, trembling. "Remember how sick I was? Remember how we said we'd try anything?"

She nodded, unable to form a coherent word or thought.

"Well we did, didn't we," he went on. "The liver was experimental, we knew that."

"Because...because of the stem cells, yes, one of the first ones grown rather than donated," she managed.

"Yeah. And also some of the anti-rejection drugs were non-standard. We were told that. A jump in transplant medicine, they said. Remember?"

Again she nodded, her mind a blank now, wondering where this was going.

"Well, it was a bit more experimental than you knew."

"What?"

He was getting angry now. "You'd only have bleated on about it not being right, and I *needed* it, Sarah! I didn't have long left, we both know that. So they used stem cells, yes, but from...a variety of sources. A bit of this, a bit of that...' He smiled, an expression intended to soothe, and that was probably the scariest part of all.

"And it worked, look!" He opened his dressing gown, and Sarah started to cry. His skin was mottled, still normal-looking in places but mottled blue and green in others. It looked wet, shiny.

She shook her head, unwilling to accept what her eyes were telling her, and Mike grinned at her. It was too wide, that grin, far too wide. And his lips, so rubbery.

"Why…how didn't I…?"

"…notice?" he asked, finishing her sentence for her. "Because I can hide it, that's why. They call it camouflage." Now his skin was completely mottled, his hair almost colourless and his mouth oh so wide… "Lizards do it, chameleons, some fish…and some frogs."

He gulped, and the sound it made was familiar now. Frogs. He sounded like a frog. Voice almost croaking.

"Jesus, Mike."

"Don't be scared," he said. "Please. It's just me." He blinked, and she noticed again that the eyelids went sideways now, the eye itself almost completely black.

"What did they do to you?" she whispered.

"They used stem cells to grow the liver, of course." His tone was matter-of-fact, in a *why are you having a problem with this* kind of way. "And it works, doesn't it? I'm not sick."

"You are, Mike, you are," she moaned. "This isn't normal, none of it is."

"Oh but it is," he said, and now he was smiling again, and she wanted to scream. "It is for us."

"For us?"

"Sure. You didn't think I'd want to go through this change alone, did you?"

Sarah stared at him, wild-eyed. Was there someone else? Surely he didn't mean...

"There it is," he said, his voice soft and downright amused. "The penny drops. Those vitamins I got for you, when you first found out about the baby?"

"What about them?"

"Not a vitamin in there, sweetheart. Not one. I got them from the transplant docs; they're quite keen to see how their little project pans out."

"So all those check-ups you've made me have, because you were worried. About the baby."

"Not really worried about the baby, no. And not really me. More that the docs were worried about how you'd adapt. *If* you'd adapt."

"Jesus! Adapt to what?"

He spread his arms wide, moved towards her. "To our new life, of course. They've been watching." His smile grew wider. "They're watching now."

There was a rushing sound in her head, and as she started to fall she realised she could hear someone, downstairs. Footsteps coming closer, and then the door was wide open and what looked like paramedics came rushing in.

"She's not ready yet? Jesus."

Mike sighed. "I was just explaining. She'll be ready, okay?"

One of the men nudged her with the tip of his shoe as she lay on the floor. She was hot, her mind racing, her stomach turning over and over as she tried to make sense of what he'd told her.

Mike leaned forward and hauled her up, lifted her into his arms. His skin was slick, he struggled to hold on to her. That smell, so familiar and yet so strange...she tried to speak but her throat was dry; she was so thirsty. Her head swam, and she felt awful – she was going to be sick if...then Mike had her. His grip was tight as he shouldered past the medics and made for the stairs. "She's just dry, that's all. She'll be fine, you'll see."

She was still screaming when the men outside started spraying them with some kind of chemical that stank; when he ran across the road and down to the river, jumped into the stagnant water, still holding her in his arms as they sank into the welcome coolness of the water.

The Harvest

By Phil Sloman

My father first told me about the forests when I was six, as his father had told him and as countless fathers had told their children for generations beforehand. It reminded us where we had come from and what could have been.

I had sat cross-legged at his feet in front of the open fire, listening to the sound of anaemic logs splitting as I waited for him to speak. It was the winter after we had lost Grandmama. Whilst alive, she would hobble across the room in that staccato manner of hers, little more than a scrawny collection of skin and bones shuffling between her chair and bed depending on where the sun was in the sky. She would remain motionless in one spot whilst the world carried on around her, waiting until it was time to move again or be moved when her strength failed her. She barely shifted even when her bowels needed voiding, decorating the inside of a pissing pot with her excrement, a pot I was responsible for emptying.

She lived an existence and nothing more. When she went my father had said it was her time and we should be grateful. And maybe he was right. But I'd still cried, too young to know any different.

We would still catch Grandmama's scent drifting through our shack after she had been taken, delicate memories blossoming here and there. On occasion I would turn to speak to her, fancying that I glimpsed her amongst the shadows, only to see an empty chair.

I wore at least four layers of clothing that night as I sat before my father. A ragged combination of mismatched hides and furs thrown together haphazardly in an attempt to keep warm. The winter had been vindictive. Blizzards screamed outside in protest, bringing biting ice to take the ill-prepared. It was all we could do to keep warm and the fire we had did little to stave away the chill.

My father sat opposite me in his cold chair, his head tilted downwards as he watched my inexperienced fingers fiddle with the buttons of my coat. Leaning forward, he tugged at my jacket, half pulling me to my feet. His calloused hands pushed the thin carved bone through the buttonhole, knitting the hides together. Every small measure counted in our fight for survival. Back then, more and more of our people died during the winters than had been anticipated. Young and old, nature didn't discriminate. *Thinning the herd* as my father called it. I didn't really understand what he meant at the time. I nodded partly to appear wise whenever he said it and partly to hide the shivers which ran through my body.

Satisfied, he settled himself into his seat, squirming on his scrawny rump in an effort to make himself comfortable. Once he was ready, and not a moment before, he started speaking in those deep, gravelly tones of his.

That was the night he first told me about the forests. And The Happening. And the night I lost my innocence.

***

The Harvest was almost upon us.

"John, is everything ready?"

I turned at Sarah's voice, raising my hand in acknowledgement as she strode across the yard. Sarah was responsible for the Harvest this year. Each year the honour passed to a new Marshal elected by the Council. Sarah had become eligible last year, after losing her mother. Her appointment had been unanimous, carried by more votes than anyone could remember.

"It's good to see you, Marshal Wilson," I said, greeting her with a gentle kiss to the cheek.

"I think we can probably manage without the titles, John," she smiled, breaking our embrace and lightly pushing me away. "We used to roll naked together in the dust bowls when we were no bigger than prairie dogs so I think you can safely call me Sarah."

She winked at me, innocently enough.

"Yes, um, yes, Sarah," I bumbled, trying to look anywhere but directly at her.

I felt a flush of colour rising in my cheeks. Years ago I had hoped we might have rolled naked together in less innocent circumstances but she had chosen Dreyfus Wilson and that was the end of things. Not that I hadn't done well out of the matter. I had been life bonded with my wonderful Esme, mother to our beautiful daughter Rebekah, who was herself blossoming into early womanhood. Yet Sarah could still make me blush like a hormonal teenager without her ever knowing why.

"Would you like to check everything is how you would like it?" I asked, trying to regain a small measure of control and keep the subject away from naked flesh.

"That would be great, John. Thank you."

She had gently placed a hand on my shoulder and turned me without my realising until we had already taken the first few steps towards the threshing sheds.

In the time after The Happening, after the forests were scorched, we had become wanderers, drifting over large tracts of land as we struggled to survive. We pillaged what we could find of use, things which had survived from the Time Before, but our discoveries were few and far between. Now and again we came upon the remains of a dwelling, a ragged wall or a collection of timbers sticking up from the ground like decaying teeth waiting to be pulled. There was never enough to build a community. That was until we chanced upon Hope. My father said it was what had been called a farmstead in The Time Before. A place to grow food and keep animals for slaughter.

Hope had been sheltered in a valley, protecting it from the worst of The Happening, leaving a derelict barn and some outbuildings which were mostly unscathed along with the main house. We rebuilt what was there and added to it from junk scavenged from other sites. In the end, as the years passed and Hope grew, we stopped searching for more materials and accepted our lot. Scavenger parties had started failing to return as they began searching beyond our usual haunts, venturing into the vast salt flats out east, known simply as the Forbidden Zone. It was shortly after the last party vanished, years before my father had been born, when we devised the Harvest.

Sarah led the way into the threshing shed whilst I followed a couple of paces behind. It was dark inside, reliant on what little natural daylight filtered through the gaps in the corrugated roof. The inside of the shed was huge, the height of at least three grown men and the length of another seven laid head to toe. Apart from us, the building was devoid of people. Everyone was outside making final preparations for the start of tomorrow's

Harvest. Several kettle drums were scattered around the edges of the shed's interior, more scavenged goods dug from the soil when our forebears had first discovered Hope. Each was of a good depth, ready to hold the crops we would collect later.

"You've done a good job, John." Sarah moved towards the darkness at the centre of the shed as she spoke. With her back to me, she missed the smile creeping across my lips. "A very good job indeed."

Sarah stopped short, within touching distance of the behemoth which dominated the centre of the building; Old Rusty. She looked so small next to him. He was a testament to the Time Before, a colossus of the mechanical ages. The barn had been rebuilt around his girth after our forebears had first discovered him.

He had been named after Rusty Shearsmith who had led the foraging party which found him. Old Rusty had been an ancient agricultural machine, a relic from the past used for the harvests in The Time Before. The bulk of the monolith was a huge hunk of metal casing which housed the belly of the beast. Faded symbols were etched into the outside in white paint but none of us had ever been able to make out what they said.

Spilling out from the guts of Old Rusty was a long stretch of metal flanked on either side by two huge flywheels. These drove the conveyor belt hidden inside, rotating it constantly to allow the Harvest to be sorted and separated into the pre-prepared drums. The original belt had been made of cloth and had frayed away decades ago. Since then we'd used old hides prepared for the purpose, pulled taut and pinned out in the main square under the hot summer sun. Each day the pins would be moved an inch further apart in order to stretch the hides as much as possible until they were ready for use. No one hide would ever stretch far enough so we would stitch together the ones we had until we had something which would do the job. We had perfected the technique so well, it was often a good decade before we had to replace the belt again.

Inside Old Rusty's belly was where the action took place. This was where he hid his cutters. The dicers and splicers. The buffers and the blades. These had been my second job of the morning after cleaning the drums. I had taken a whet stone to each blade and worked them carefully until they were perfect, ready to take the crops of the Harvest. Only the most trusted members of the tribe were given this privilege and it was my honour this year.

Over the years we modified Old Rusty to be more precise. Originally we had fuelled him with thick, black oils found abandoned inside the old barn. When these ran out we devised a way to power Old Rusty with oils we pulped from the crops we harvested. As well as the fuel, we modified the blades, tweaking them so each cut yielded the greatest gain, leaving nothing to waste. We had existed with so little to survive on in some years that everything about the process needed to be perfect. The belly was the most important part of Old Rusty. This was where the crops were separated into grains, stalks and chaff. It was all made use of. The grains for food, the stalks chopped and used to stuff our bedding and the chaff compacted for fire logs. Everything had to have a purpose.

Sarah patted the side of Old Rusty and stepped back.

"You can be proud of yourself, John. You really can."

She placed her hand on my shoulder in a show of appreciation, leaving it there a little longer than I felt comfortable with, before making her way to the open doors of the shed and the daylight beyond.

***

The next morning was the day of The Harvest.

Everyone was excited. This was a day of celebration. This was when the village came together to embrace life and look to the year ahead.

The sun was shining brightly with a warmth which reflected the smiles on the faces of Hope. Everyone was dressed in their finest clothes ready for the festivities to begin. Hair was plaited into strands and tied back with dyed pieces of leather. Men, women and children marked their faces with coloured streaks of mud, two lines drawn enthusiastically across their cheeks.

The entrances to each shack were decorated with

coloured stones laid out in the dust before them. Each formation showed an ellipse surrounding a small spherical stone. They were tokens for the Gods, a representation of the all-seeing eye looking up at them with reverence whilst they looked down on us in judgement.

Jowah, our priest, had risen early to perform the blessings for the Harvest, dressed in his ceremonial robes. He had delivered the ceremony of The Cleansing in the threshing shed behind closed doors, preparing Old Rusty to receive The Harvest. Jowah was one of the few people allowed to go into the shed unaccompanied. Years back, fanatics had attempted to destroy Old Rusty days before the Harvest. There were two of them, Peter and Martha Nordstrom. They had argued Old Rusty was an abomination to nature, that we could and must live without him, that we were forfeit to evil if we didn't destroy him. It was only by the will of the Gods that they had been discovered before it was too late.

George Fitcherton came upon them as they crept into the shed, intent on tearing Old Rusty apart panel by panel, blade by blade. Within five minutes the whole village had been stood at the door to the shed, raised by George's clamouring, and the Nordstroms were never seen again. The children said Old Rusty had got them, and that probably wasn't too far from the truth.

The damage to Old Rusty had been minimal and it had taken less than a week to get him back into action. It was the one and only time The Harvest was held late and it had been followed by a fallow year.

But the past was the past.

Today was about the future.

A large mound of heaped earth had been gathered together in a circle in the centre of the village, the summit levelled off to create a platform of sorts. It was wide enough for six folks to stand upon and about the height of a man's waist. The banks had been compacted and decorated with the same stones used for the entrances to our homes. It gave the impression a multitude of eyes were following you no matter where you stood.

The whole village gathered expectantly in front of the mound, waiting in anticipation for events to begin. My father was there with me, as was Esme and our daughter, the four of us caught somewhere towards the middle of the throng. Rebekah was drawing looks of annoyance from a few of the older members of the village as she jostled to try to get a better view of the platform.

An excitable buzz of conversation filled the air. Parents were telling their children about the first time they had attended the Harvest and how thrilled they had been to see the offerings. Old timers were recounting how things had been better in their day, less of this pomp and circumstance, and how far too much fuss was being made as it was. My father wasn't one of them. He remained his usual taciturn self, standing with arms folded, gazing ahead at the sky above the platform. *'Only speak when there's something worth saying'*, had been his motto, and he had always been true to his word.

Mixed in amongst the general buzz was a more distinct hubbub as Rebekah continued to fight for a view. From the best I could tell, she had managed to elbow Patty Tomkins in the stomach who, in turn, had spun round to give Rebekah a strong piece of her mind. I was about to step in when the pair of them stopped. It wasn't just them who fell silent. All around us conversations were dying. Making her way towards the mound was Sarah, flanked by her guard of honour.

It was Sarah's duty to open The Harvest, as it had been the duty of all the Marshalls going back to Rusty Shearsmith's time. She was dressed in her ceremonial outfit, hides dyed a dirty green with the leaves from our crops and a metal chain looped around her neck, part of Old Rusty which he no longer needed. She wore an unassuming headdress made from dark feathers scavenged amongst the bushes of the scrublands.

One of the guards offered his hand to help her to the top of the mound but she waved it away, ascending the slope with a simple grace. Standing at the summit, she steadied herself, brushing down her clothes as she prepared to address the crowd gathered in front of her. Sarah raised one arm to head height, her palms turned out with her fingers pointed skywards, signalling it was her turn to speak.

"My friends," she said, looking across the spread of faces as the silence of the crowd became complete. A mixture of young and old, male and female gazed up at her expectantly.

Even Rebekah had settled herself, eager to hear what Sarah had to say.

"My friends," she repeated, "it is good to see you all here on this day of celebration. I feel privileged to have been elected your Marshall this year. It is a responsibility I wear with great pride and great humility. I am honoured to be able to stand before you as we come together in recognition of all we have achieved this year, and to look ahead to all we will achieve in the coming year."

A murmur of approval ran through the crowd.

"Each year we realise more than we had thought possible. The soils get richer with each passing season and the crops more plentiful. When I was a child we would never have dreamed of the bounties we will receive today. Truly we are blessed and the Gods recognise all we have accomplished together."

Sarah paused and looked to the skies, her skin pulling taut as she craned her neck skywards. She sketched an ellipse on her chest with the tip of her finger, the nail scratching across the coarse material of her gown. As one, the crowd followed suit, each of us marking ourselves, casting our heads back and muttering individual thanks to the Gods above for their mercy and benevolence.

Things might have gone differently that day if I had taken more notice of my father staring dolefully at the ground rather than the ceremony before me. He had been doing a lot of that lately, simply standing and staring, either at his feet or off into the distance. None of us could ever pinpoint the exact moment when he changed but in hindsight it was easy to see the signs; a hindsight which would never restore our pride.

Sarah clapped her hands, breaking us from our prayers and bringing us back to mortality.

"Jowah, please." Her voice carried easily above the renewed murmurings as excitement overtook the village.

We all smiled, watching Jowah emerge from his shack on the edge of the square. His censer drifting nonchalantly back and forth as he approached, trailing smoke behind him. It had been made of an old metal can found in a raiding party and each Harvest Jowah filled it with acrid smelling thorns gathered from the scrublands.

Jowah was old, entering his fiftieth Harvest. He had the scars to prove it. His hair was grey and hung wispily across his shoulders. Bits of peeling paper-thin skin could be seen on his scalp in the places his hair struggled to cover. His family had always performed the necessary rituals of the village, keeping Hope safe from the whims of the Gods. When the time came, his son Jedwah would become priest in his place as tradition dictated.

Two guards gave him their arm to help him up the mound, causing amusement from some of the younger members of the crowd who didn't understand the afflictions of age. They all received stern looks from their parents who would no doubt find extra chores for them later.

"Dear friends," mumbled Jowah, his voice low, almost inaudible as he positioned himself next to Sarah on the mound. The crowd moved a fraction forward, everyone leaning in a little closer as they strained to hear his words. "Dear, dear friends. Today is a blessed day. A blessed day indeed."

"Speak up, you old coot," muttered Rebekah next to me. She turned to glare at me as she felt the rough of my hand clip the back of her head.

"Respect your elders, young lady."

She gave me a feisty look before turning back to the ceremony.

"It is with great deference that I stand here as one with you all," continued Jowah, ignorant of our family spat. "To offer our gratitude to the Gods for the bountiful crops provided to us since our last Harvest."

This year had been a good one, as had most in recent memory. Even as Jowah spoke, there were two fields worth of crops beside the threshing shed ready to be processed. These were truly prosperous times.

"And as a sign of our devotion, we give to you our tithe that you may see fit, in your wisdom, to grant us another year of riches. Children, would you please come forward."

Four of the younger children shuffled towards the mound, glancing back at parents who offered reassuring gestures and smiles. I remembered when Rebekah had been eight and chosen to be part of the ceremony. The sun had been fierce that Harvest and her cheeks were ruddy beneath her fair hair. She wouldn't go up without Esme holding her hand, the other grasping the garland we had prepared for her.

The sun wasn't so hot today and the children were more confident than Rebekah had been, although I thought the Harlow child, barely six years old and all freckles, looked like she would burst into tears if the wind blew in the wrong direction. Like Rebekah had done, each child carried a garland woven with leaves taken from the crops we had harvested. Under Jowah's instruction, the children formed a line in front of the mound, bumping against each other until he was satisfied they had the right of it.

"Three, two, one," conducted Jowah behind them in hushed tones.

On cue all four raised their arms, holding aloft their garlands for everyone to see.

"We honour those who have given to Hope," they chimed in unison, remembering the words practiced for hours with their parents. "Who will continue to give to Hope and who have always given us hope."

They all took a bow, the Harlow girl waving excitedly at her parents now that the hard part was over. These were the rare moments we treasured amongst the hardships of the year.

"Thank you, my four little ones. Splendid. Truly splendid. And we have four more members of our clan who deserve recognition today." Jowah signalled out across the crowd with his arms, beckoning people forward. "Four of you who have seen this village grow over the years. Four of you who have given so much in support of Hope and we ask you to give one final time. Step forward and be recognised, Rachel Thornicroft, David Thornicroft, Susan Brinklow and Patrick Morton."

I looked up with pride at the sound of my father's name, the last of the foursome to be called. This was the most important honour to be bestowed on a member of the village and I couldn't have been prouder. I turned in expectation to embrace him, but he was already moving through the throng towards the mound, his back facing me. I made a vain attempt to grab his shoulder but he was already beyond my reach.

"Father," I shouted, cupping my hand to my mouth, trying to make myself heard above the general excitement of the crowd. "Father, I love you."

For one second I fancied I saw him stop and half turn his head in my direction but then he was swallowed up by the crowd as they resealed their ranks around the passing quartet.

At the front, the elders received a garland from the children, bowing down to make it easier for the youngsters to drape them over their necks. Once the last garland was given, the children ran as quickly as they could into the anonymity of the crowd and the proud embraces of their parents with a gentle ripple of applause rising up around them.

The four elders were centre stage with the sun shining full on their faces. Each of them stood tall and proud, facing the adulation of the village. The Thornicrofts were together hand in hand, David towering over his wife. Next to them was Susan Brinklow, or Ma Brinklow as we had known her as children. She was the best cook in the village, creating tantalising meals from the limited crops available. Every now and again we would capture a careless bird or rodent, or a gondril if we were really lucky, and she would set about baking mouth-watering pies. Finally there was my father, the person who had made me the man I am today. His expression was gruff as ever, never one to show his emotions. It would have been nice to see him smile, today of all days. Even when Rebekah had been born he had done little more than give me a pat on the back before setting out to work in the threshing shed. I hugged Esme and Rebekah close to me, an arm around each of them, as I beamed with pride.

Sarah took over from Jowah, towering over the elders gathered in front of her. All four of them had seen more Harvests than anyone else in Hope.

"This year marks the sixtieth Harvest for each of you," announced Sarah. "We thank you for your service."

"We thank you for your service," repeated the crowd as one.

"We thank you for what you do today for the good of the village."

"For the good of the village," echoed the crowd.

"And through your sacrifice you will live on with us forever."

"With us forever."

Hands went to chests as we made ellipses with our fingers before sinking to our knees in reverence to our elders. It was tradition. It was what the Gods required of us and it kept them happy for another year. In my father's words, this was where we thinned the herd. It is what he had explained to me those three decades gone and had stayed with me ever since.

"Jowah, please make the final preparations."

Jowah's head bobbed up and down in a jagged motion as he signalled his charges.

David was first, making his way to the top of the platform with more vigour than I would have credited him with. A cheer went up as he reached the summit, composing himself between Sarah and Jowah.

"I am ready," he said, his deep voice sounding out strongly across the kneeling crowd.

Jowah turned to him, his finger dipped in ash from his censer, and marked him with the all-seeing eye on his forehead and then his chest. He hugged him like a brother, far more firmly than I would have thought he was capable of given his slender frame, and whispered into David's ear. These words were always kept secret between the priest and the elder, a final message to take to the Gods.

Jowah stepped back and presented him to the village. Tears were running down David's cheeks, a big smile across his face as we offered another cheer to celebrate his life, pumping our fists to the skies.

And then my father ran.

He was halfway across the village before anyone realised he had broken, sprinting round the edge of the gathering. Someone tried to block his run. Marcus Westbury I think it was, a slip of a lad, with barely fourteen years to his name and not strong enough for the task. Marcus was on his backside before he knew what had hit him. Feral beasts are always stronger than you realise.

I was up and running before I knew what I was doing, Esme and Rebekah staring after me in bewilderment. The rest of the village was starting to react, getting up from their knees to see what was happening. I could hear Sarah shouting instructions to her guards. Jowah was wailing to the Gods to forgive us, to understand this was the act of one man and not the village. Esme and Rebekah were calling after me but the words were lost to me in my confusion.

The rest of the village watched as I dashed to the edges of Hope after my father. I could see him flagging as I made up the distance separating us. It was only a few strides before I would be by his side. I was still hoping he would see sense and stop. Tell me it was some sort of misunderstanding. But he didn't. I pounced.

The ground hit my chest hard as I dived at his feet, but it caught my father worse. He was down before he knew what was happening to him, my arms wrapped around his ankles. His face took the full force of the impact, grazing up against the rough dirt on the edge of the village.

Conflicting feelings of hope, elation and fear tore at my thoughts and my heart as I lay in the dirt panting for breath, but the overriding emotion I felt was shame. It was rare for anyone to make a run for it. The last time had been Michael Forson, at least twelve Harvests back. It was always the ones who thought they deserved more time, the ones who had decided to put their needs above the rest of the tribe. I was embarrassed for my father. I would never have taken him for a runner. The man I thought I knew would have walked up to be blessed with honour, ready to become one with Hope. He should have gone with honour instead of the shame which would now haunt every mention of his name.

I couldn't even bear to look him in the face as I rolled him over and sat upon his chest, straddling him with my legs to stop him from escaping. This should have been our proudest moment together, a son helping his father give back to the village but the moment was gone now forever. He looked at me, pleading for forgiveness. There was a heat behind my eyes and I struggled to focus. Tears of shame ran down my cheeks as I felt the rough hands of the guards dragging me away.

***

One guard took his shoulders and the other his feet as they carried his unconscious body into the threshing shed. The tips of his fingers brushed the dirt of the floor as they hung limply by his side. This was a further embarrassment to add to the shame he had brought upon our house. The rest of the elders had walked through the shed doors, their heads held high after receiving their final blessing from Jowah. My father barely made it in without brushing his backside against the earth. I hoped when my time came I would carry myself with the dignity and self-respect demanded.

Old Rusty dominated the interior, commanding the eye to his magnificence, drawing the ear with the sound of his chuntering engine and clattering blades. The large kettle drums were positioned at the end of the conveyor belt. To the side of Old Rusty, the Harvesters were waiting for my father; three villagers given the honour of continuing years of tradition. The first two Harvesters were Mary Rand and Albert Shingle. I was the third.

The Harvesters had two roles. The first was the cleansing we had carried out the day before in preparation for Jowah's blessing. Here and now began the second.

I was the newcomer to the trio, this being my first year. I was taking on the responsibility from my father as he had from his father. He had spent the past year training me, almost as soon as the last Harvest had been completed. Together we must have covered each technique, each ritual a thousand times over until I was ready to take on his mantel. When Sarah, as Marshall, had awarded me the Harvester's mark, three scars cut into my right forearm, neither my father nor I could have been prouder. It felt like a different time and place now.

The three of us stood in readiness next to a big metal bath, another find which had come from a different settlement. It had taken four men the best part of two days to bring it back to Hope but the effort had been more than worth it.

Each of us held a small hand sickle by our sides, blessed by Jowah and brushed with sanctified dirt as part of the cleansing ritual. The sickles had been crafted from blades taken from Old Rusty and set into thin white handles. In the early days the cuts they made were crude and rudimentary, but decades of refinement had turned our knife work into an art form.

The guards dropped my father's body at our feet, a couple of steps to the left of the bath. A low groan escaped his lips but he remained unconscious. At least it meant he wouldn't bring any further shame to me. Mary stripped his limp body of all his clothing, removing his shoes, jacket, vest and trousers before piling them in the corner. The clothes themselves would be cleansed and then placed on the mound in the centre of the village for those in need who could claim them for their own. Property was fleeting in Hope, passed on to others for the greater good.

Once my father had been stripped, Mary and Albert lifted his wrinkled body between them and placed it into the tin bath.

He had been a tall man, a head taller than most in the village, and his arms and legs stretched over the sides of the container. His head lolled backwards at the top end of the tub, exposing the withered wattle of his neck.

The ground scrunched as I shuffled forwards. I hadn't been trained for this moment. Everything my father and I had rehearsed meant nothing now with him presented before me like this. I could feel Mary and Albert's eyes looking at me expectantly, waiting for me to do what needed to be done. All the while Old Rusty thundered away behind me, willing me on. My arm felt heavy as I raised it and brought the blade across the bulge of my father's throat. I let the steel rest reluctantly against his skin as I built up the strength to perform my duty.

It shouldn't have happened this way. The rest of the elders had walked to the bath themselves. They had taken the blades and placed them against their own throats, uttering one last prayer to the Gods before delivering the killing stroke. I was sickened with embarrassment by what I had to do. One further unexpected failing from my father at the end.

Part of me hoped he would come to and grab the blade from my hand before dragging it across his own skin. The other part of me wanted him to stay unconscious so he couldn't see the shame in my eyes. That part won as I let the blade slip across his throat.

Blood flowed quickly, running in rivulets down his neck and coursing along his spine. It pooled in the base of the bath, mingling with the blood of the other elders until it was indistinguishable from the rest.

Eventually the gushing slowed, the rhythmic spurts becoming sporadic and weak before reducing to a trickle. And then it stopped. I took my father's head in one hand, tipping it back even further than before. The cut at his neck responded, opening wider to create a dark pit across his throat. It looked like an exaggerated second smile, leering at the world as if it were sharing one final joke where only he knew the punchline. Lifting the blade again, I started working on his scalp.

My touch was delicate; the strokes administered with great care and attention so as to not nick the flesh underneath. Clumps of grey, lifeless hair fell to the ground, ready to be collected up and placed into the pre-prepared drums. We lifted his body from the tub and placed it on the ground, working away at the areas which had been submerged in blood.

We removed the pubic hair, curly and grey, shaved from around his member as well as the hair I'd removed from his chest and armpits. All of this was his chaff, the stuff which would normally be thrown away. All of it was placed in the drums. Later it would be compacted into blocks with the inedible husks from our grains and held together with mud. We would stack these into log piles, combined with the logs we made from our own hair collected throughout the year, ready for fuel for the dark winter nights to come. Once my father was bald all over, Mary and Albert started their work.

Their cuts were precise. The first blade was inserted just above the sternum. The metal sliced easily through his weathered skin as it was worked vertically down towards the groin. With the main incision made, the second blade was introduced, the pair of them working together in tandem as they set about removing the skin. It took less time than it would take a man to run round Hope three times. They stopped halfway through to flip the body over, hanging it across the blood-filled tub to let any residual fluids drain into the mixture. Half the blood would be dried and made into sweet tasting sausages. We could store them for months, eating them as treats when the mood was on us. The other half would be poured across our fields, fertilising the soil and giving life back to the land the Gods had seen fit to grant us. It was more than coincidence that the crops had grown stronger year upon year since the first Harvest all those decades back.

The skin which my father had spent six decades inside was split into four sections and thrown in a pile with the skins from the rest of the elders. They would be dried and worked on by the seamstresses of the village, to be sewn together. We made use of cultivated shards of bone for needles, lacing them with tendons which we had harvested for thread. They would marry them up with the hides of the prairie dogs and gondrils we hunted, and work them into the clothing we needed.

With the skin removed, we turned our attention to the meat underneath. There was an art to removing the flesh and separating out the choice cuts. The parts not fit for human consumption would be used to lure the vermin nesting out in the scrublands to provide more food for our pots. Some of the meat would be consumed at The Harvest feast this evening, small morsels provided for the village to remember and celebrate the sacrifice made today. The rest would be packed in salt taken from the plains of the Forbidden Zone and eaten sparingly through the year.

Then we were left with the bones. These would be given to our carpenters to form furniture and tools for the village. When we had first settled here, we raided the incumbent graveyards which had been filled with bodies from well before The Happening. Those bones were weak and shattered easily. It was only when our own people started dying out from old age, disease and malnutrition that the Gods blessed us with the wisdom to make best use of their death-delivered gifts.

That was back before we had discovered Old Rusty and The Harvest had been devised. In the initial years of The Harvest, we had fed Old Rusty the whole corpse, choosing the old and the lame. The idea of using cadavers for resources was firmly established by then, this was just one step beyond. As my father always said, you did what you had to in order to survive. Eventually rules had to be agreed. We ran out of the elderly faster than we had anticipated, indiscriminately charging anyone with being incapable when the winters felt too cold and meat was needed. The lame, it was argued, often healed and those who were truly diseased were not fit to be used and had been deemed unworthy by the Gods. Finally the village council, led by Rusty Shearsmith, had agreed that only those who reached their sixtieth year would be selected. To keep track, each year from birth we would all be marked with a scar on our inside thigh so there could be no dispute as to a person's age. This was part of The Harvest ritual now. First was The Blessing, next came The Harvest and finally The Marking whilst the feast was prepared. No one ever willingly added an additional year.

By all accounts, the early Harvests had been messy, wasteful affairs with bodies being sent through with mixed results. This was before we considered the use of sickles. Mostly we had been able to retrieve a selection of meats from the conveyor belt but more often than not these were contaminated by ruptured bladders or burst bowels brimming with rotting food and faecal matter. What bones we had been able to rescue were broken or fractured, of little use beyond making handles for the tools we needed. The skins were always mangled and shredded, useless for the needs of our village.

Over time we introduced the Harvesters, skilled men and women able to make the best use of the materials presented to them. We taught them to use the blades, to Harvest the best flesh and to preserve the skins. In this way, Hope was provided for and the Gods received their sacrifices, albeit in an amended fashion.

Only a few people knew this new truth. Old Rusty was

a totem, something for the children to be scared of; and some of the adults too. Crime was punished with a quick trip to the threshing shed followed by a feast for the village. Ours is a very honest society. More importantly, none of us could be seen to be more involved than we were. Old Rusty had been provided by the Gods in our hour of need. He was their vessel and needed to be treated as such. The bond made with him and the sacrifices needed to be seen to be immutable. Our presence would muddy this clarity for some, raising questions best left unanswered. It was better this way.

We still used Old Rusty. Even now we had the two fields' worth of crops to be threshed and sorted. These would be used to feed the village. And there would be more throughout the rest of the year, enough to create stores over the winter and see us through for a good two years if necessary. It had been an age since we properly needed the meats from the Harvest to survive.

The Gods still needed their tithe though.

Three pieces of flesh had been prepared and were ready to be used, one slice each from Rachel, David and Susan. The meats were still wet and twinkled under the paucity of light which made it into the shed. They would be given to Old Rusty as an offering to the Gods before the crops went through. These had been hacked from the elders when they were still alive, to symbolise the giving of living flesh.

There was one tithe missing.

For the second time that day, I could feel Mary and Albert

looking at me with a mixture of pity and expectation. It was ordained an offering had to be made from each sacrifice but it wasn't so simple. My father's flesh was sullied by his actions, not fit for consumption by the Gods. We would be condemning ourselves to a fallow year. We had seen it before over the years, impure flesh punished with diseases which had almost wiped out our crop supply and our village. Almost.

"We'll make it quick," said Mary, compassion and understanding weaved throughout her words as she approached me with Albert at her side.

I looked at them and shook my head. Albert cocked his head, his eyes asking if I was sure. I nodded. This was my shame now, I had to make amends.

My blade made a crescent in the earth as I placed it by my feet before struggling out of my vest. The exposed torso was dark underneath, not as weathered as my father's but it had seen its fair share of hard labour beneath the harsh skies. I let my fingers explore my body, grabbing at bits of flesh; my breast, my arms, my gut.

Bending, I stooped to retrieve my sickle, feeling the coldness of the bone handle in my grip. Be quick, be quick, be quick. I repeated this to myself like a mantra, over and over, as I readied myself. And then I cut. Deep.

Crimson flared across my vision and I passed out before I was done.

***

The sound of thundering blades greeted me as the world came back into view. Crops were being thrown into Old Rusty and carried deep into his guts. My breast was wet and exposed. Mary or Albert had finished the job for me and left me there. More shame for me to carry.

Lying crestfallen in the dirt, as Old Rusty whirred away behind me, ripping the husks from the sheaths, separating the crops into food for the village, all I could do was think back to the evening of the winter after my grandmother had been taken. I pictured my father sitting looking down at me, the logs crackling in the fire as he adjusted the hides hanging off my shoulders. I remembered how snug they had felt and how much I loved my father in that moment as he settled himself into his bone white chair waiting to tell me about the forests. That moment was ruined now forever and I hated him for it.

Transcending Nature

By Stephanie Ellis

"Imagine a world without the scarring of masts and satellites. Imagine a world where electronic information can be transmitted easily and without a break in connection. Imagine a world where communication transcends nature..."

John's eyes glazed over as the advert played out on the giant plasma screen. The words had once meant something to him a long time ago but he had left all that behind. Around him, people rushed to and fro on their way to work or whatever destination urgently demanded their immediate presence.

"John, John Carter? It's you isn't it? Really you?"

John automatically turned towards the voice calling his name. The face in front of him was familiar, yet he couldn't quite place him.

"It's me, George. Drake. Remember?"

Grey eyes looked at him hopefully for a sign of recognition. "Uni, remember?"

Aah, university. So long ago now, thirty, forty years? A time he knew he had enjoyed, a time of big ideas and hope. He remembered him now. The only one from their group to make it really big.

"Oh, *George*. Yes, yes, of course I remember. It's been a long time." The man in front of him was the complete opposite of himself, the scent of money contrasting strongly with his own unwashed state, although he much preferred his own honest stink.

"Too long," said George. "I often wondered what had become of you."

"Oh, things happened…life, you know – stuff."

George ran his eyes over John, not bothering to be discrete about his appraisal.

"Look, I've got a while before my train. Why don't we have a coffee, catch up?"

"Sorry," said John. "Can't. Things to do, places to go…"

He was surprised to see a look of disappointment on George's face when he had expected relief.

"Oh. Never mind then but…here's my address. If you're ever in the neighbourhood, just…you know."

George handed over a card and then turned and quickly walked away. John didn't even look at it, just crumpled it into his pocket.

The following weeks continued in much the same manner. Nobody ever noticed his daily visits though as they passed by, all plugged in, wired up, tuned out, citizens of cyberspace in preference to reality. Communication wasn't advancing, it was dying.

And John finally opted out, becoming a permanent member of the ranks of the destitute.

That was when they came for him, the welcoming committee that visited all new arrivals. When they found George's crumpled business card however, the beatings stopped. "How do you know him?" asked one.

John did not answer. A kick in the ribs prompted him.

"An old friend."

"Yeah," sneered his attacker. "Then what you doing here?"

"Taking a little time out," said John. He received another blow at that.

"Well unless you want to take some permanent time out, I suggest you give us your name."

The heel of a boot ground into John's hand, making him cry out in pain.

"Oops, sorry mate. Didn't see your hand there, I do tend to get a little clumsy at times. Always getting told off for it. Oops-a-daisy, now I've trodden on the other one."

Unable to take any more, John yielded. And then everything went black.

When he came to, he found himself lying in what appeared to be a hospital bed with the screens pulled round. A careful glance down revealed restraints had been applied.

"Ah good. I see you're awake." The curtains had been pulled back and George now stood over him.

John tried to speak but found even that was beyond him.

"I'm sorry about...this," said George, indicating John's prone body. "We had to restrain you for your own good; it was the only way to give you the treatment you needed. Now rest some more and we'll talk later. The tranquilisers should have worn off by then. And John, I am sorry."

George disappeared, leaving John angry and none the wiser. He tried to move again but unconsciousness claimed him once more. The next time he awoke he found himself in a small bedroom; white-walled, white-curtained, white everything. This time he was not restrained. Gingerly he climbed out of bed and made his way to the window. He could see nothing except trees and fields. Wherever he was, it was not in the city.

A nurse entered his room.

"Where am I?" he asked.

She merely gestured he was to follow and led him down long softly-carpeted corridors and into a small lobby. Low-lights and pastel colours gave the place a muted, tranquil atmosphere.

"Take a seat," she said. "I'll let Mr Drake know you're here."

John sat, or rather sank, into one of the chairs; he rubbed

behind his ear which seemed to be aching slightly.

A number of journals had been left there to occupy any person waiting. All scientific publications of some sort, the type of material that he had once been extremely familiar with.

A door opened and George came forward to shake his hand. "You have no idea how pleased I am to see you here, and looking much better than on our last meeting I might add." He seemed to ignore John's bruises.

John kept his hands to his side. He still felt the after-effects of his recent beating, something in which George obviously had an involvement.

"Ah, yes. I am sorry about that little incident. Some of my people get somewhat...over enthusiastic. I had hoped you would get in contact with me before, avoid all...this. Things have moved on greatly and I really need your input." There was a worried look in George's eyes.

"What line of business are you in now?" asked John curiously. "You always were a bit of a dabbler from what I remember - a lucky dabbler though, whatever you touched seemed to turn to gold. We used to call you Midas."

"I remember," said George and handed John a business card with a smile.

John glanced down. Midas Industries. He laughed despite the situation, his ribs protesting violently in response.

"I've actually been developing a field you were working on before your...um..."

"Breakdown?" offered John helpfully.

"I've always wondered what triggered it," said George. "What made you walk away."

"Simple. The technology was moving too fast, people were pushing me, wanting results without proper testing, always pushing. I got scared of the future. I didn't like what I saw coming."

John had hated that time. His one golden idea had turned to dust in front of him. Since then he had heard vague rumours that Midas Industries had picked up his research. *Imagine a world that transcends nature*, those words had come from Midas.

"You were right," said George wearily. "We moved too fast. I'll show you."

"I'm not sure..." said John. He had suddenly gone cold, the old fear returning.

"I *need* to show you," said George. "I need your help. And this time you cannot walk away."

George led him along more corridors and into a room which acted as a viewing platform to a circular laboratory below. Monitors ran around the walls with a central carousel containing a master computer. A transparent cubicle was located in a space in the lower half of the chamber. There was a man lying on an operating table. John recognised him. One of his fellow vagrants. The man's eyes were open but they were glassy, staring up at the ceiling with a vacancy that was unsettling.

"Is he dead?" John asked.

"No, merely sedated."

"Is that what would have happened to me if they hadn't found your name in my pocket?"

George shifted uncomfortably.

"So you bring people here against their will to do what exactly?"

"To make a useful contribution to society."

"And how is that achieved?" asked John although by now he could guess the unpalatable truth.

"Your *TranSend Project*. You had a vision of a truly sustainable society, where humans could generate and harness energy from their own bodies, where they could create a communications network without scarring the land, where every person was a self-contained nett contributor to a human internet."

John remembered. It had been an idealistic goal, an impossible achievement which had resulted in the deaths of two volunteers when they had submitted to the implants he had created. That was when he had walked away.

"Look." George indicated a small scar behind his own ear.

"You carry an implant?" asked John in astonishment.

"Never ask anyone to do anything you would not do yourself," he said with a grim smile. He turned on a monitor in the room and immediately it homed in on George, creating an image of the man on the screen. A little red dot appeared where he had indicated the implant was located. So far it was as John recalled. Then he noticed something else, tiny little fibres projecting out from the implant.

"What's that?"

"A...modification that we added to your original design," said George. "It's a nano-fibre, we embedded one into each chip before it was inserted into the subject. We had found that these fibres increased the uptake of electrolytes from the body's fluids, boosted the bio-battery that operated the chip. It stopped the breaks in transmission that your early tests suffered from."

"Looks as though you've cracked it then. I mean here you are, walking around, perfectly healthy. The Midas touch again." John was unable to keep the slight note of resentment out of his voice. He had made the breakthrough in this particular field but his pioneering work had been marred by lack of funds, misfortune and ultimately death. Then along comes George and everything's rosy. "You must've made a fortune."

"Not too shabby but..." George broke off and walked over to the window. John followed him and stood at his side, noticing how his old friend had rested his head against the cold glass and closed his eyes to everything around him.

"We've...we've recently discovered a side-effect which so far has proved irreversible. It affects everybody who has had an implant...including me."

"Then for God's sake why are you bringing in more...?"

Realization dawned. "You're bringing in the people society won't miss to try and work out what went wrong. They're expendable. You were going to do that to me!"

John was furious, furious at himself for being the trigger in all this, furious that people had died because of him, furious they were still dying.

"John, we could argue over this all day and all night and still we wouldn't get anywhere. You've worked with this technology. Come to the labs, help us put it right."

And he would, or at least he'd try. John knew he did not have any choice.

"What exactly is the side-effect you were talking of?" asked John, keeping his eyes fixed on the vagrant below.

"Those little projections you see around the implant, the nano-hairs, they were created from an organic, cellulose-based material. We discovered they replicate themselves and as they do so they extend their length and 'hitch' themselves to the body's neural pathways. I haven't had the implant long so mine are only recently developed. To be honest, me having the implant was meant to be purely a publicity stunt to show investors how much faith I had in the project. Until that point we had inserted implants and not really looked too closely at the feeder hairs."

"Feeder hairs?"

"Oh that's what the 'tecs call them because they keep the battery fed, keep the chip going."

"What made you finally sit up and take notice?"

George tapped another panel on the screen and a report came up. They were patient reports, one in particular, Patient X had been showing extreme paranoia to the extent he had to be permanently restrained. That was when they examined the fibre structures more closely, started to study the effects of their interference on the mental state of the individual. The nano-generators were taking too much of the body's sodium and potassium ions via the feeder hairs that just sucked them up like a straw. A strong chemical imbalance had been created and the brain seemed to short-circuit on a regular basis causing worrying psychotic episodes.

"That's not all," said George. "Come."

He led John out of the room and down yet another passage. Peering through the grill in each door, he could see they were all occupied by something that looked human except that each inhabitant was covered in a silvery sheen, a coat of very fine silver hairs. "We do have one very extreme example," said George and led him on down to a cell that unlike the others had mostly clear reinforced glass walls.

In the middle of this room was again a table with a figure on it. It looked human, it had the same shape but the outline was becoming somewhat blurred by the cloak of silver fibres covering it and...unlike the previous cell occupants these fibres were longer and had melded into the entire surface of the bed.

"Is he still alive?" asked John, horrified at what he saw.

"We think so."

"You think so!" exploded John. "Surely you know?"

"There is still brain activity and his eyes show he is still aware of his surroundings."

"Eyes?"

"For some reason they are the only part of the human body which the fibres ignore. They leave the optic nerve completely alone."

"And that is what you will all become?"

"Yes."

John looked again.

"I don't understand how those fibres have become so thick. If they are based on nano-technology then we should not be able to see them."

"As they replicate they thicken, they twine themselves not just around the nerves but around each other. They have an organic base which, in the presence of electrical impulses, gives them life at the expense of the host - it's a truly bizarre parasitic relationship. When the fibres are exposed to air they form a protective shield that nothing can get through."

"What do you mean - nothing?"

"Fire, acid, bullet. You name it, nothing gets through."

"And how exactly did you test this?"

George didn't answer, again his silence spoke volumes.

"We need to find a way to reverse this process or cure the subjects but we need to do it – discreetly."

"Why discreetly?"

"Some of our sponsors are from the military, they seem rather excited about the properties of this nano-material. It is they who want the implants to continue. And I don't, not at that price." George indicated the prone figure once more.

John sighed, feeling the weight of the old despair pressing down on him. He had started all this.

"If I can help I will. Could you let me in to take a closer look at the subject?" He nodded towards the operating table.

"Unfortunately that is impossible. Please...look again though, tell me what you see."

John peered through the glass, noted the solitary table and the figure on the bed. One part of the chamber was slightly in shadow, the part where the wall was not transparent, he had ignored this before. A chair was positioned against its surface and there seemed to be someone seated on it. Fibres ran in the direction of this figure from the patient on the bed and probed at the seated body, digging in to the flesh, sending pathways up to the brain, covering the face in a veil of silver.

"She was a nurse," said George. "And one, I must add, who had *not* received an implant. Once the fibres break the surface of the subject's skin they start to move towards the nearest human. It's just like iron filings being attracted to a magnetic source. I've never seen anything like it."

"Sounds like this happened more than once," guessed John.

George led John back to his office in total silence.

"You have access to everything related to this research. I'll leave you to read it over. Nobody will disturb you. I'll be back once I've done my rounds."

"Just one thing," said John. "You talk about it as an infection."

"Because that's exactly what it is, gradually snaring everyone that comes into contact with an affected person into its web and at present there's no stopping it."

The web had taken over the world once before, a virtual reality into which humans retreated as soon as they discovered it. Now a physical web was appearing and people were rapidly disappearing into this as well. Would they notice any difference? Would they mind? Perhaps this was just the next stage in the downward spiral of human evolution.

George left John to the papers stacked in front of him. Slowly he started to read through, ignoring the sandwiches that had been left for him, allowing his coffee to go cold. He turned on the laptop and looked at the plan of the site. The papers explained how the transmitters embedded in each human generated a signal allowing all to be viewed and tracked. He tested it out on the laptop but the voyeurism made him uncomfortable. He turned off the camera view, he did not want to see people. Instead he focussed on the red dots that blipped everywhere. Some were moving but others remained stationary. These were the ones who were in an advanced state of transformation. Their signals were stronger than those whose implants, like George's were relatively new.

He focussed on the room which contained the patient now conjoined with the unfortunate nurse. The 3D imagery showed the path the fibres were taking from the prone body to the seated figure. All moved up towards the brain and showed signs of strong electrical activity. Zooming in again, a scan of the woman's brain came up. It was now emitting the same signal as all those who had received the implants. Yet hadn't George said that she had *not* undergone that procedure?

He scanned through the papers again, looking for the details of all those who been infected in the same manner, checking to see whether they were supposedly implant free or not. Then he pulled up the site plan once more. He studied the staff who had come into contact with the fibres erupting from their patients. There was no physical movement but again huge electrical activity and all of them showing the same brain signals as emitted from their patient's own implants. The fibres were somehow replicating the nano-generators themselves, continuing to build up the circuit along which they ran.

He rubbed distractedly at his neck and then he noticed the sore point behind his ear once more. And he knew, with a sudden dreadful, furious certainty, what it was. His finger hovered over the button on the laptop screen which allowed you to flip to transmission monitor view. He closed his eyes and pressed. When he opened them again all he could see was the glowing red dot. And it was at that moment that George walked back through the door.

"You bastard," hissed John, hurling papers and computer to the floor, only just stopping himself from attacking George.

"I couldn't take the risk that you would refuse," said George calmly. "A vested interest would mean you would have to help."

With effort, John restrained himself. For the time being they had to work together. Revenge could come later.

"Your initial assessment?" asked George.

Fighting back his loathing, John explained about the victims who had transmitters created in their brains via the feeder hairs. What he needed to find out was what the pulses generated meant. Was there some sort of communication going on between the victims and if so was it human or was it something to do with the nano-generators? And why were the eyes left unaffected? The eyes were the window to the soul but would he be allowed to look?

"There is no way you can get near them without being caught," said George when he asked.

"Then we start with those who have not reached that level," said John. "Sit down."

"Why?"

"So we can gaze lovingly into each other's eyes. What do you think!" snarled John. "The generators are all about communication, the fibres about feeding that communication circuit, keeping it going, linking it to others. Perhaps we could read something from each other, I don't know. It's not a scientific theory. Just something I want to try. Now, as in the words of every third-rate hypnotist, look into my eyes, focus on the implant in your head and the transmitter in mine. See if anything happens."

The two men sat and stared at each other. Initially John felt stupid and embarrassed and then reality fell away and he was somewhere else. Bright lights pulsed around him, waves of energy coursed through his body, his thoughts, his mind was being pulled in one direction. It was a struggle to stay in control. An image flashed across his vision, he was somewhere else reading a newspaper. Then it changed again and he was stood up and saluting an officer. With an effort he tore his eyes away from George.

"What did you see?" he asked shakily.

It took a while for the other man to reply but he too had what they called 'other body' experiences, although he had seen different images.

"You wanted a human communication network," said John eventually. "Looks like you've got one."

"Could we try this with others?" asked George.

"Maybe but I have one more thing I want to test before we involve anybody else," said John. He wanted to know who was in control, where the real nerve centre was.

They returned to the glass medical bay. All other personnel

had been banished from the area. Two guards watched them on the monitor.

"All very *Twilight Zone*," said George dryly. "I remember you were a big fan of that series."

John ignored him. "Now remember, we can't look into his eyes from here but we can focus on his brain."

"You don't want us to hold hands?"

John laughed despite himself.

"I think I can give that a miss," he said.

They moved to the glass and stared down at the man, trying to shut out everything else from their senses. It wasn't long before the same visions of light and energy flashed into view. Fighting the temptation to pull back he forced himself to continue. Down he went into a network of wires, trying to read what information was being pulsed back and forth. This was different to his experience with George. In this world were wires and chips, digits, monitors. Suddenly he was looking out of a computer screen and not just one but millions. He was looking at the world. He tried to pull back but it was hard, every time he dragged his eyes away, a fresh pulse of energy would propel him forward. Electricity arced through him and he could feel his muscles going into spasm - and then he lost consciousness.

When he came to, he found himself lying on a couch in George's office. George himself was lying on the opposite sofa. Above them a nurse hovered anxiously.

"What happened?" he whispered hoarsely.

"The guards said you both seemed to be having some sort of epileptic fit. They're being treated in medical now."

"Medical. Why?"

"They were electrocuted when they touched you, received quite nasty burns."

"What about Mr Drake?"

"He came round a little while ago. Now I don't want either of you to move until I can get a doctor to you. I'll be back shortly."

"What happened, John?" George's voice sounded weak, distant.

"I believe we got into the central nervous system of the circuit. I saw lists of names. But I don't understand..."

"They're all the ones who have had an implant or been infected," said George with a sigh. "They're imprinted on my memory and I couldn't forget them even if I wanted to. You could call it a registry. We seem to have become part of an organic computer."

John raised himself very gingerly and went over to George's laptop. With all these energy bursts zooming about he needed to see if there had been any more internal changes to them both. He flipped the webcam on and set it to scan before pointing it in George's direction. He could see the wires were now running further into his central nervous system. Drake frowned when he saw that, he obviously had not expected such a difference.

"Try it on yourself," said George.

John put himself under the eye of the scanner and immediately noticed that what would have been minute protuberances were now at least an inch in length each.

"The rate of replication has speeded up," said George. "Perhaps because we linked ourselves to the others, received some sort of energy boost?"

"Perhaps," said John, trying to ignore the impression of energy waves that was currently pulsing across his field of vision. "How do you feel?"

"Terrible," admitted George. "I seem to be suffering double vision at the minute. If you'll excuse me I'll go and lie down."

Left on his own, John found it wasn't only images he was seeing. Voices were coming through too.

"Hello, hello. Major Johnson, can you hear me? Corporal Everly reporting from Observation 1. Subject has...sorry sir, our equipment is malfunctioning. Electricity spikes the engineers say. Sir, sir..."

John could still hear him screaming even after the transmission had ended. Then it was followed by another and another. Information was bombarding him from every angle and whilst this was happening he could see the wires growing within his body. If only he could think in peace and quiet, try and focus.

A communication network needed power to keep going. Power was supplied by a generator, in their case by human generators but the network needed more than that – for the present at least; if it was left too long there would be sufficient numbers to form an autonomous network and it would be too late. If they could cut off the electricity supply to the site would that give them literally, the break they needed? He could not afford to wait, he doubted if George would ever wake up again.

Information was being streamed through him. The network was demonstrating organic traits in terms of growth, reproduction and feeding but where was the intelligence?

It was strangely quiet as he walked the corridors. There were no guards to stop him and he reached the generator area unchallenged. He called up the entrance code from a memory which did not belong to him. The control office was empty.

Swiftly he moved to the desk, to the lever that would stop the nightmare. He reached forward to press it down but as soon as he made the slightest contact he was sent flying backwards by an arc of electricity. Groggily, determinedly, he got up and tried again. This time the blast was stronger.

There was something else at work here; here was that intelligence.

John glanced around the room, grabbed a jacket that had been left behind by someone and wrapped it round his hand. Then he tried again. Through the jacket his hand clutched at the lever, pressing it down as power surges shocked his body. He could smell something burning. Then it suddenly all stopped. The room went dark, a few small lights continued to flicker in standby mode but apart from that there was nothing. The pulsing images that had seared through his brain had stopped. The screaming voices silenced. He had done it.

But then guards appeared, refused to listen, pulled him away.

"Better get the power back," said one. "Big game tonight, don't want to miss it do we?"

A few minutes later the site was once more ablaze with light and sound. Messages started streaming through the wires, data flew through the air.

John felt it all. Every pulse, every wave, every binary digit attacked him, searing through his body, into the brain, homing in on the cerebrum, pounding him with information. By the time they eventually got him on to a bed, he was completely exhausted, overloaded in a way he had never before experienced. He tried to close his eyes but they refused to shut, they had become monitors for his now virtual world. He tried to move an arm, a leg but neither limb followed his commands. He attempted to speak but his mouth wouldn't open. From the angle of his head on the pillow he could see one of his arms, the sleeve rolled up, showing his exposed flesh. The skin had taken on an almost translucent appearance. Something was shimmering just beneath.

The lights around him dimmed to their night setting. He gazed in fascination at his arm that now rippled and sparkled in their reflected glow. It was strangely hypnotic, beautiful even.

There was something he was supposed to do but he couldn't quite remember what.

Creeping out from the building, fine silvery tendrils wove themselves around body after body, stilling movement, stifling freedom. Every victim that was added contributed to the sum of human knowledge in this mass database. Receiving all this data, the once human lying in the window-lined bay of Midas Industries Research Institute decided it was time to perform a little light housekeeping. Instructions to delete corrupt systems and defrag others went zipping across globe. Slowly eyes started to close, links were broken and names were removed from the registry.

Communication had indeed transcended nature.

Idle Hands Are Grist To His Mill

By Adrian Chamberlin

"There is not one of you who does not have a jinnī appointed to be his constant companion.' They said, 'And you too, O Messenger of Allah?' He said, 'Me too, but Allah has helped me and he has submitted, so that he only helps me to do good."
– Sahih Muslim, Book 39, Hadith No. 6759

"... 'the Hands' – a race who would have found more favour with some people if Providence had seen fit to make them only hands, or, like the lower creatures of the seashore, only hands and stomachs." – Charles Dickens, *Hard Times*, 1854

What good are hands when the fingers have been cut away? It was not the first time Altair had pondered this, for his father had often cried out in anguish over his fate - but the thought now had terrifying immediacy when the sobbing boy was dragged away from him, his only friend crying the very same words his father had uttered so many years ago.

The other children barely hesitated before resuming their duties in the sea of cotton beneath the treacherous weaving looms, not even the barks of the overseers required to get them back to work. This was not the first time they had seen one of their fellow Parish Apprentices maimed by the industrial instruments that provided meagre sustenance for them and fat profits for their guardians. It was not the first time Altair had seen the merciless machines of the cotton mill feed upon its workers, either, even though he had been in the workhouse less than two months.

But it will be the last, he thought when he stared at the blood on his workhouse issue shirt. The coarse material could not soak it up quickly; pools broke and dribbled around the buttons. On the looms, however, the cotton continued its journey, the scarlet-drenched strands disappearing and replaced with new white ones. As though the accident had never taken place.

It was not this that made Altair's mind up, it was the bewildered expression on Matty Benshaw's face when the boy realised the beseeching hands he'd clasped onto Altair's shoulders would not maintain their grip. The cry of despair was barely human, something a small wounded animal would make.

All fingers and both thumbs gone, severed at the metacarpal joints, maimed for life, but Matty's first words upon this realisation were: "How can I work now?"

Barely whispered, almost inaudible over the incessant roar of the spinning mules and the ceaseless thunder of the shuttles ordering the threads. But those words carried their own thunder; Altair heard nothing else.

Finally, the storm. Altair turned to the spinning mules, ignored the snarls from the overseers and went to find Matty Benshaw's fingers.

***

Where does night truly begin?
  His father's words, a riddle with no answer. *Why do I recall this now?*

It was always too easy to give the wrong answer, to be misled by the question. Where, not when – every child knows *when* night begins. But how many adults know *where*?

An answer began to form when he stared at the sky above the workhouse and its adjoining mill. The clouds of smoke from the mill's chimneys never dispersed during day time, and hastened nightfall; the day ended unnaturally early, by artificial means. The night was welcomed here; a refuge from the sights and sounds of industrial horror, a respite from the grinding toil that hastened the workhouse's charges to early graves.

The stench of the infernal day remained, even though its clouds of ash and smoke had departed. A sickle moon shone in the cloudless sky, as thin and pale as Matty Benshaw's white face after the accident. Shocked into bloodlessness as the rest of his blood rushed to leave his body by ten freshly opened pathways. A lifeless sky? *No, there is something more to this riddle...*

The stars were out, and his eyes were drawn to the constellation Aquila. Its brightest star Altair - his namesake – still had not reappeared.

Altair looked over his shoulder at the darkened workhouse and the adjoining cotton mill. The red brick was softened, almost a pleasing pink in the corrupted moon's light.

Almost.

To Altair – and to every Parish Apprentice who entered its doors, whole of flesh and hopeful of spirit with the prospect of learning a trade – the masonry was the colour of blood. The house was bloated with the life-fluid of the orphans just as the owners and overseers were bloated with the wealth their charges' labour brought them. Night did not hide its crimes, nor soften them.

The window he had climbed down from was still open, no candle light illuminating the interior, and he imagined the faces of his dormitory companions peering through, both jealous of the Arab boy's decision to escape but fearful – even dismissive - of his chances of success.

No light. Good; the alarm had not yet been raised. He turned back, considered the path to his freedom. The landscaped gardens and striped lawns of the mill disappeared behind the red brick walls, replaced with the rutted cart tracks of the road leading down to the harbour village.

Pale light from the jumbled fisherman's cottages hid behind wood smoke trickling from crumbled chimneys; the smoke did not disperse because there was no breeze.

Fairlight Bay was nothing more than a cove formed by a pincer of jagged cliffs that swallowed sunlight and soaked the wind; the few fishing boats that remained here could only leave by rowing past the southernmost point and then tacking for an age before meeting a full wind.

Running away to sea, just as his father Tariq had done from a distant land so many years ago. Tariq had told him once that the terrors of the sea were nothing compared to the forces that brought destruction and death to the parched deserts of their homeland. Even the blood and fury of sea battles were preferable to what they had escaped.

Altair wondered if that was why his father had brought them both to Fairlight after the wounds incurred at Trafalgar made him useless to His Majesty's Royal Navy. The lack of wind was a curse to the fishing industry, but would have been a boon to the man haunted by the roar of the sirocco and the horrors it brought.

Only for new, man-made horrors to take him. Fishermen were unwilling to take in a man with such a foreign countenance, despite the prevalence of non-born Englishmen in the Navy – and they certainly had no use for a man without hands, nor his dark-eyed, motherless son.

To the workhouse with you. They don't require full bodies there; it's all grist to their mill....

Altair's eyes moistened and he sniffed. Away from the machine house, where family did not exist, he was overcome by the thought of community below, of loving mothers and fathers, familial bonds that even poverty could not break. How alien it would be to him, a boy who had no recollection of his mother, let alone memories of both parents together...

He wiped his eyes and snorted, angry with himself. This was no time to be plagued with thoughts of what he'd never known. He was in one piece, had his health and...

...all my fingers and thumbs, unlike my father. Unlike Matty...

Unconsciously he rolled his fingers, turned his hands into fists and squeezed. He relished the feeling of pressure, the sensation of fingernails digging into palms, the warmth that flowed through them...

Until he realised the fists were powered by fury. Hatred,

fuelling rage at what his adopted country did to its young. The clouds drew their black curtains over the moon and consigned him to darkness.

And in the darkness, the sounds of the night became louder. A solitary owl hooting; the scurrying of something in the grass of the verge; the molasses-thick breakers of slag-filled water sliding on the shingle beach below. Whispered words in a tongue he didn't understand but recognised. The language of the deserts of Arabia, borne by the wind...

Wind. He felt a chill, realised the coolness that turned the beads of sweat on his forehead to ice crystals was brought by the very thing that never visited Fairlight.

A wind from the south, across the sea whose waters hissed and roared in the bay below, as if the ocean shuddered at the wind's touch. The words a chant which grew louder, roaring in his ears, louder than the engines and looms of the cotton mill but not deafening.

Energising. He felt the power of the words even though he did not understand them. Images of destruction filled his mind and he exalted in them – the workhouse and its mills, crumbling to ruin and falling into the sea; the hated machinery that ate flesh and drank blood and shat money, ripped from their mountings and smashed to pieces; the men who profited from the inhuman misery raised into the night sky by the winds and torn to bloodied shreds by the demons who rode the sirocco.

It did not matter if the slaughter and devastation

continued long after the mill was rubble and its owners blood-drained sacks of meat. It was a righteous anger that possessed him, not a rational one. A primal force from before man's creation of dehumanising machinery and exultation of profit before humanity. Let it tear this land and the empire it birthed to pieces, consign the demons who wore starched collars, top hats, and mutton-chop whiskers back to the hell they surely sprang from.

This, the chant delivered with his father's voice promised. In return for...

He looked back to the headland, to the mill, and the ancient structure that adjoined it. He put his hands in his pockets, felt the small, fleshy bundle in the damp handkerchief.

It's all grist to the mill. A curious expression, meaning: 'nothing is wasted, everything can be utilised for a profit.'

Nothing would be wasted of Matty Benshaw's fingers. What profit would be gained for what he was about to do with them was unclear.

Perhaps repayment is a better term. He had a new direction now. Not to the sea, but back inland, to where the wind would blow once more.

***

Like Altair's father, Matty Benshaw need not have worried about being unable to work. The workhouse found uses for all bodies, whole or not. Able-bodied was a term that did not exist here.

Daydreaming when you should have been paying attention to the machinery; you have only yourself to blame. Your hands may now be as idle as your head, but we'll find a use for you. Where you're going you can walk in the clouds to your heart's content...

And Mr Dawkins was true to his word. There were six others on the treadmill, all men. They could have been in their twenties, or their fifties, it mattered not, for poverty and toil had aged them all: turned the stubble of their scalped skulls grey, deepened the lines on their foreheads, stripped the flesh from their bones, hunched their shoulders and bowed their backs so they resembled maimed sewer rats curling into balls and resigned to death. They paid each other no heed, just stared with dulled eyes ahead through the soot-encrusted windows at the view of the headland and the windmill.

The handrail before them never felt the grip of fingers or the gouging of nails. Each man had lost at least one hand prior to assignment to the treadmill chamber, and when exhaustion overcame them they slumped against it, attempting to find relief by resting what remained of their arms upon it before the remorseless screw of the cylinder tread forced them to stand again. Sweat was the only movement on the men's faces, beads of salt water emerging through the grime like blisters, and the smell of fresh sweat soon merged with the stale odour of yesterday's, and the day's before.

The chamber – it may have been a hall or a storage facility at one point, Matty knew not – echoed with the heavy tread of the walkers' wooden clogs on the corrugated iron cylinder, the only sound the overseers allowed. Not that the men were of a mind to talk anyway; their grim expressions were identical: tight-jawed, unsmiling, their eyes squinting as they tried to focus on the open skies denied them.

It was a cruel thing, this vision. Even though greasy clouds of smoke from the chimneys of the adjoining cotton mill roiled past the windows at irregular intervals, momentarily obscuring the view, the sight of the grassy headland and the disused windmill intimated another world, denied the walkers forever. Doubly cruel to Matty Benshaw, who often walked in the clouds in the sanctuary of his head and now trod an eternal trek toward clouds he would never reach.

The windmill - over a hundred years old, maybe older; it had been disused long before even George the Third and his madness took the throne - was a reminder of a time when wind was in abundance and manpower was not required to grind wheat or generate electricity.

The headland terminated in grey skies, the sea below obscured from view. Matty wondered if this was what made the men maintain their punishing pace: an unconscious desire to march toward the cliff edge and hurl oneself into the sunless sky, to imagine for a brief moment that one had escaped, was free as the birds that no longer flew in the bay, before plummeting to the slag-encrusted rocks below to meet their end. Freedom of a sort.

Fly...it made Matty think of the silent Arab boy, the only one who had rushed to his aid. The one who helped him with his studies when the schoolmaster towered over the huddled children in the coal shed that passed for a school room, demanding answers to questions the orphans didn't comprehend, and gleefully administering the cane in response.

The Arab boy was the only one who never cried out when the birch struck his knuckles. Not that the schoolmaster ever had a valid reason to strike him; Altair knew how to respond to the questions, gave calm, measured answers that were as eloquent as they were factually correct, which made Mr Dawkins hate him even more and lash out regardless. 'Valid reason' be damned.

The schoolmaster refused to call him Altair, even though it was the only name he had, the only one he knew. He was renamed Alastair, though that was a first name and implied undeserved familiarity in an environment where everyone was known by their surname.

Matty never forgot the first exchange between Mr Dawkins and the newly-arrived orphan. The dark-eyed boy had a curious air about him, one that spoke not just of exotic climes and a heathen upbringing, but also a sense of timelessness, as though an ancient spirit travelled the land, disguising himself as a small boy who had not reached twelve years of age. He had lost his father and was alone in the world, yet hid his grief in a manner Matty had envied; he himself had not stopped crying for almost a week when his mother passed on.

Mr Dawkins's eyes were hollow and his skin pale. The frock coat hung loosely on his shoulders, and his starched collar flapped around his thin neck like the wing of a dead seagull. Dark circles besieged his small, dull eyes; he appeared to regard the world through black, eyeless holes.

Altair? Sounds a filthy Mohammedan name, boy. What does it mean?

It comes from *al-nasr al-tair*. It means Flying Eagle. It is well known in the west: it is the name of the brightest star in the constellation Aquila, in our Milky Way. That too means eagle.

The brightest star and *a flying eagle?* A wheezing laugh and a sneer. *Your Saracen parents had high hopes for you, did they not? Will you fly from here, boy? In a land where there is no wind, how can you soar above us? Will you shine the brightest, as Lucifer did before he fell?*

When the time is right. When the winds blow again and sweep the filth and decay from the land. Then I will soar...and shine.

Even Mr Dawkins looked disturbed, the authority wiped from his face. A giggle from Matty had the schoolmaster turn on him in fury, a new target for his impotent rage.

The cane struck myriad blows, and Mr Dawkins's face turned a mottled red, his teeth bared, sweat beading his upper lip.

This amuses you, Nefelibata? Another ingrate mocks me with fantasies and dreams, and you doubtless see him as a comrade in arms! I'll give you both something to laugh at...

And all the while Matty kept laughing, the pain not registering, and the Arab boy stared at him in a strange, appraising manner, mouthing the name Mr Dawkins used as an insult. Repeatedly, as if the name was a charm.

Nefelibata...Nefelibata... Nefelibata...

The punishment began the same day. After the three-hour tutorial and religious instruction was over, when the other children shuffled, dead-eyed, to their dormitories, Matty and Altair were summoned to the courtyard.

Each night, while the other children slept, Matty and Altair were tasked to pick oakum with nothing but cloud-dimmed starlight to guide their fingers. Only when the chapel bell emitted two chimes were they permitted to head to their cots, their fingers numbed and bleeding, their bodies chilled with the night air, to rest for a few meagre hours before the bell struck six times and they joined the other children for another interminable day beneath the treacherous cotton looms.

Matty, why does he call you Nefelibata?

It's Greek, I think. Means Cloud Walker.

Cloud Walker?

Yes. Daydreamer. He hates stories, flights of fancy he calls them.

An insult that is a badge of honour, I think. We are of the same branch, my friend. You dream by day, I by night.

What d'you mean?

Look to the sky, Matty. Do you see the stars? That cross there: that is the constellation Aquila.

I can't make it out. It's so dim.

Yes, it is. Because the air here is corrupted; the demons of industry try to smother the light of the Heavens. My father told me that in the desert night each star of Aquila once shone like a precious gem.

And Altair is the brightest? Which one is it? I can't see it.

Altair's head sank. *No one can. It no longer shines.*

Only on the second night did Altair tell him of why his father had run from the desert. The tale of demons that murdered his wife and hungered to consume Altair sounded just the sort of fantastical tale that would have Mr Dawkins fuming. In daylight, Matty would have struggled to believe it. But at night, with the dimmed stars and a struggling moonlight, and no sound but the unearthly creak and groans of factory machinery cooling in the night air, it felt real.

I grew up on an English warship. I became a powder monkey – a child who ferried parcels of gunpowder to the guns on each deck, while my father served with valour and distinction as a midshipman. It was after the storm at Trafalgar - when my father lost his hands - that the light of Altair disappeared from the sky. My father sank into despair when we came to London; he believed the demons from the desert had stretched across the sea to make England their playground...and a man with no hands cannot fight.

That was too much. Trafalgar was twenty years ago – Altair would be in his thirties now. But what did it matter? If it was fiction, it was a good one; Matty's mother would have delighted in the fantasy. The memory of his mother, wasting away to a skeleton after consumption took her from the cotton mills had made his eyes water. Seeing this, Altair put a brotherly arm around his shoulder.

My father once said: "Where does night begin?" I am certain the answer is close at hand. I look to the night sky, waiting for a sign. We shall be delivered, my Nefelibata, and reunited with our lost ones. I promise.

What had started as a punishment had now become a reward for the two boys. Alone in the world, the Cloud Walker and the Flying Eagle stared into the night and awaited a sign.

Matty's mind cleared, and the present took hold. He saw the iron skies above the headland, the static sails of the windmill, and knew no birds would fly here again. The flare of comfort burned out, turned into a cold ball of iron that sank into his stomach and to compliment his ever-present gnawing hunger rather than replace it.

Hunger and pain, the only companions on the treadmill

who spoke to him. The ache in his ankles and his thighs, the encroaching stiffness of his knees, the soreness of his sockless feet in the ill-fitting wooden clogs – all these were welcome because they were new pains, and they distracted from the ache of his mutilated hands.

The pain had its own rhythm, in tune with the movement his body made on the treadmill. Right foot forward and all pressure – and pain - put on the left side of his body, momentarily easing that of his right. Then left foot forward, and the process reversed.

And through it all the men remained silent, nothing but wheezing and stentorian breathing to counter the harsh grinding of the treadmill cylinder. What did it power? Was it to grind wheat and corn into flour like the windmill would once have done? Or did it generate electricity? No, that wasn't it – it was steam from burning coal that powered the mill's spinning mules.

What, then? Matty glanced up to the face of the man to the right of him, tried to read the man's thoughts through the facial fog of evaporating sweat and old dirt and constant despair. Did this man once question the treadmill's purpose, and then dismiss the matter as unimportant?

The man's right hand gripped the handrail easily, casually; his left arm hung at his side, the wrist a rounded nub of hardened flesh, mottled by grime. The stump looked older than the man's face, and Matty wondered how old he'd been when he lost his hand. *Was he my age? Has he been on the treadmill since then?*

The treadmill would be here long after Matty was gone. Other feet would replace his. Other maimed hands would attempt to clutch the handrail, allow their memories to fade, replaced with a vision of empty skies and the false promise of freedom. This realisation created tears, which blurred the view of the headland and the disabled windmill. His body wracked with sobs, made his balance on the treadmill precarious, as though the earth moved beneath them all, a giant stomach growling in anticipation of its next meal of exhausted, maimed corpses, meat tenderised by inhumane toil and seasoned with despair.

***

He didn't remember the end of the shift, or the sparse meal of broth that tasted of nothing and left his hunger untouched, or the cot and its filthy blankets his exhausted body fell into. He didn't remember waking and shuffling through the corridors of the workhouse to take his place on the treadmill.

But he remembered the dream. For once his sleep had not been filled with half-formed images of the mother and father who died in the gender-segregated dormitories of the workhouse before he was six years old. His slumber had been filled with the windmill: the round tower's fresh whitewashed masonry gleaming in the bright midsummer sunlight, the sweeps of its four sails painted a pleasing bright blue to match the cloudless skies. The sails turned briskly but smoothly, the millstones that nestled comfortably within the warm bowels of the tower coming to life and going about their work with joy.

Joy. He'd actually *felt* that. As though he'd been part of a machine, but one different to the iron-shod monstrosity that held him prisoner.

No, he realised in the cold dark of day. Not the machine itself. Stones and wood relied on power as all machinery did, but this was more natural. In keeping with the forces of nature, working in harmony with them. One of the most ancient and elemental sources of power, one which never made its presence felt in the slag-clogged site of the cotton mills.

Wind. Fresh, clean, invigorating; bringing the salt scent of a sea that had not been corrupted by slag and ash and clinker and turned into the River Acheron Mr Dawkins's lectures on Dante brought to mind. And with it, the creatures that owned the skies returned. Gulls turning lazy circles above the headland, bellies content with the plentiful fish below; tortoiseshell butterflies adding a further splash of colour to the gorse bushes on the headland; bees languidly moving in the breeze to honeysuckle to foxglove to daisy, pollinating and producing food. Giving and receiving, a fair exchange for their labour.

And above the scene of nature's splendour, the highest

of them all, a solitary eagle soared. A Golden Eagle, a rare sight indeed on the southern coast of England. It swooped above the fantail and alighted on the open window in the mill's cap. It folded its wings gracefully and disappeared into the darkness. Moments later it emerged, a tubular piece of flesh in the steel scimitar of its beak.

Matty blinked at the sight that greeted him and his fellow Hands. The mockery of the window and the desolate heath it showed, the iron skies untouched by flashes of gold from the majestic eagle in flight, and the lifeless windmill. Forever stilled.

"No," he whispered as the clogs began their tattoo, the harsh symphony of wood-clad flesh and screeching iron. His legs moved in unconscious and perfect harmony with the other treadmill walkers, the stiffness and pain returning but unnoticed.

"No," he said, louder this time, crying his resistance to the removal of the scene of nature's beauty and majesty, the destruction of hope. His resistance took physical form: his clogs scraped on the raised ridges of the corrugated tread cylinder as he back-pedalled. Angry murmurs came from his fellow walkers at the need to increase their pace to make up for the boy's dragging.

"NO!" His balance was upset and he reached for the handrail. Once again his hands betrayed him; only phantom fingers encircled the iron, and the metal scraped the tops of his maimed hands. Pain speared each ravaged knuckle and fresh blood seeped through the torn and filthy bandages.

The pain was a spur. He turned, leapt from the treadmill. He landed badly, his ankle twisting and his clog disappeared into the treadmill screw's housing. The mechanism screeched in fury, as piercing as the cry of the eagle.

The granite floor seemed to tremble beneath his feet and the roar of the damaged mill screw sounded like the bowels of Hell had opened.

They opened long ago, Matty told himself as he limped to the side door and pushed it open with his elbow. Air possessed by coal dust and smoke filled the chamber and he staggered through the industrial miasma. As ever, no breeze meant the chimney smoke sank and clung to the ground, and the few people not at work were silhouettes in the smog, hunched and shuffling like the broken things they were.

Only the overseers, spilling from the treadmill chamber, moved more actively, yet they were in no hurry to apprehend the escapee before he disappeared into the manmade mist; they sensed his direction, knew it even before Matty did.

There was only one path leading to the cliffs, the windmill, and the sheer drop to the waves below, and they waited patiently for him to run straight into their idle hands.

***

Only one section of the workhouse was worse than the treadmill chamber. The Punishment Room inflicted no manual labour or physical retribution but a week in there would have the strongest willed begging to return to the treadmill and the overseers' truncheons.

Matty had heard of it, of course; all Parish Apprentices whispered of its victims in the night hours when, despite physical exhaustion, sleep lost its war against despair and departed the human battleground. Yet none knew where in the workhouse it was, or who had been incarcerated there. A legend, a myth, Altair had declared. Fear created from a phantom by the workhouse administration, a further means of control over its charges.

He was wrong. The Punishment Room is very, very real. Matty realised this when the overseers marched him toward it, felt the fear in their hands that trembled on his shoulders. *Even the Guardians are scared of it.*

There was a cruel irony in the Punishment Room's location: the very windmill in which he had experienced visions of wonder, the structure he had intended to run to.

Mr Dawkins was waiting for him. What little daylight shone on the workhouse had reluctantly decided to creep through the small barred windows of the mill house: all was gloom and dust, a fitting backdrop for the schoolmaster.

He stood by the beech-panelled casing which held the twin millstones, immobile and caked with ancient dust; he drew a skeletal finger along the runner stone and held it to the meagre light afforded by the opened door and examined it with a quizzical expression. He cracked a thin smile when the overseers brought the trembling Matty in. He rubbed away the millstone dust between dry fingertips.

"One does so despair of the ingratitude shown to your betters, Benshaw." Mr Dawkins's voice was muted, the tower masonry and its dust soaking his words. They did not travel through the cylindrical housing, did not rise through the open grain hoppers through which the thick upright shaft travelled to echo among the cogs and great iron wheels of the sail machinery.

He coughed; grey sputum flecked his cravat, and topmost layers of dust freed themselves from the millstone. "Who else would find work for a crippled lad? You would not even be able to pick oakum now, so we found you gainful employment in other ways. What remains of your hands may grow idle, but your legs will not. And you repay us with sabotage."

"Sabotage, sir?"

"A wooden clog thrown into the machinery...*literally* sabotage. A jest at my expense, hmm? You would use my teachings against me, is that it?"

"I don't know what you mean, sir. I didn't mean to damage the machine, I just wanted to...to..."

"To escape, yes. The second attempted runaway in as many days. You and the Mohammedan lad were thick as thieves; the Board of Guardians apportions equal blame to you both."

The reference to Altair made a small flutter of hope in

Matty's chest. Mr Dawkins noticed it, and a cruel smile broke on his features.

"You will note I said *attempted* runaway, Benshaw. He was returned to us this morning. The good people of Fairlight Bay know the prosperity of their village lies with the industry we provide, not the blasphemous untruths of an Arab mudlark."

Mr Dawkins pressed the attack. His dead eyes momentarily brightened with twin gleams of malice, became corrupt pearls. "The undertaker's sub-contractor in Dorchester has informed me that the coach to his establishment does not pass here until Wednesday, so you will at least have the time to say a proper farewell to him."

The wooden floor titled beneath Matty's feet. His head spun and he staggered into Mr Dawkins's arms. The schoolmaster gripped his collar and dragged him to the far end of the mill tower where a cluster of rotten flour sacks lay, mouldering. Mr Dawkins pushed Matty's head down, inches from the highest sack. Matty's nostrils filled with a ripe, sweet and putrid odour that had nothing to do with milled grain or mildew.

Altair's winding sheet. A burial shroud composed of ragged hessian. Matty tried, unsuccessfully, to close his eyes before the schoolmaster pulled the sacks away.

"Flying Eagle indeed," the schoolmaster said with a sneer. "His soul is doubtless soaring above the eyries of Hell, looking for his father. Tariq, I believed he called himself; Morning Star in English. As the Book of Isaiah reminds us: '*How you have fallen from Heaven, O Morning Star, Son of the Dawn! You have been cast down to the Earth, you who once laid low the nations! But you are brought down to the grave, to the depths of the pit.*' As his father, so too his son."

Matty could have reminded him that in Revelation, Jesus too referred to himself as the Morning Star. That Altair had explained his father's name, how respected Jesus was as a prophet in his religion; to be named after the Christ was a high honour.

But all he could think of was the horror of what had befallen his friend. Altair's flesh was a mottled purple-green due to the marriage of putrefaction and bruising. His jaw protruded in several places, and blood tracks on his chin traced the last movements his teeth had made after leaving the open wound of his tongue-less mouth.

"Our neighbours are not as enlightened as we," the schoolmaster continued. "They heard him uttering strange words, believed it to be a curse. That is why his tongue was torn away."

Red tinged the grey of Matty's vision. His head pounded. "They must pay," he snarled.

"Oh, none of the villagers performed such horrors. So they told us. He was merely found like this, and no one knows who the perpetrator is. Doubtless some ne'er-do-well from the mills, or some itinerant labourer. So they told us, and who are we to dispute the good word of our neighbours?"

Mr Dawkins's words were distant, and Matty turned to find the schoolteacher had retreated to the threshold. The door stood open, the iron sky of twilight waiting for him.

Then it closed, and Matty Benshaw's long night began.

***

"Where does night truly begin?"

Matty's head jerked up. Despite his situation, exhaustion had overcome him and he had sat with his back pressed to the locked door, as far from the corpse of his friend as possible. Knees drawn to his chest, unable to clasp them with his fingerless hands, his head rested on them until the spoken words took him from the dreamless blackness.

Beams of moonlight discoloured by coal smoke strained through the small door window, and coated the hessian-covered corpse with tarnished pewter. The stubble of Altair's cropped scalp glittered like black diamonds.

"Where does night truly begin?"

Now fully awake, Matty recognised the voice which spoke the words. But they did not issue from Altair's lifeless lips, even though they could come from nowhere else.

"Remember my father's riddle, my friend? Last night he gave me the answer."

The dead boy's mouth remained motionless, a ravaged wound agape in horror at the violence done to it. The flour sacks did not move to denote a rising and falling ribcage of expanding and contracting lungs. The sightless eyes were fixed on the ceiling.

I've gone mad. Or I'm still asleep, having a nightmare. Matty shrank back against the locked door.

"You are not mad, and it is impossible to have a nightmare worse than the one you are living in. Your salvation is at hand, my Nefelibata, as I promised. I too was scared when my father spoke to me -"

"Your father's *dead*!" Matty screamed to the corpse. "As are you!"

The scream wracked his soot-caked lungs and he fell to a fit of coughing, each one more painful than the last – not least because each stab of pain reminded him he was awake, fully conscious, and Altair's voice was real. Imprisoned in a disused windmill with a dead boy who would not accept his condition.

"I *was* dead. Now I am alive. *Truly* alive. As you will be soon. Did you not feel the connection, Matty? The vision of the windmill you are imprisoned within, cleansed of the filth of the workhouse?"

Matty hesitated.

"The eagle that flew above the coast. And the wind it soared upon. How clean and fresh it felt..."

*The eagle. Altair, the Flying Eagle...*no, this was madness.

The Guardians would have him taken to Bedlam tomorrow.

"You are not insane, Matty."

"You reading my thoughts isn't proof, Altair. All it shows is that I'm having a conversation with myself."

The disembodied voice chuckled. "I thought the same when my father spoke to me. I was in the same situation you find yourself. How did I accept the truth? Proof, of course. Let me show you what he showed me. Then you will believe."

The air filled with the beating of wings. Freshly disturbed dust roiled, glittering silver in the moonlight. Matty looked up. A patch of darkness descended from the machinery above. It alighted on the great spur wheel above the mill stones, its talons gripping the giant iron cog with a sound like the clash of swords.

It stretched its wings and the moonlight vanished. Within the darkness, two black shining pearls above a crescent that gleamed moonlit-steel regarded him steadily, dispassionate. Analysing. Judging.

Expecting.

"This is my *qarīn*, Matty. A *djinni*, the spirit companion every human has on this world, which protects its soul from evildoers. Only when one has departed the mortal shell does one see it."

"A...guardian angel?" Matty could not pull away from the unearthly stare of this strange raptor. Despite the poor light, he was in no doubt this was the same eagle he had seen in his vision of the uncorrupted headland earlier. The hooked beak stirred another memory.

... a tubular piece of flesh in the steel scimitar of its beak...

There was no sight of it now. A chuckle came from wherever Altair's words generated.

"A guardian, yes. An angel? That is open to debate."

Matty looked from the empty beak to the torn bandages of his maimed hands. An unspoken request entered his mind - a psychic connection between the ethereal raptor and him.

The image of eight fingers and two thumbs, the ten lost phalanges, and a new use for them. The eagle was hungry.

But I have nothing to give you.

The eagle squawked. An earthly cry, one that intimated physical hunger.

"That is not true, my friend. Come to me."

In a daze, Matty approached the makeshift bier. He felt no fear of the corpse now. He knelt. The combination of mildew, mould, and fleshly putrefaction assailed his nostrils.

But the latter smell did not come from Altair. A different aroma emerged from him, a subtle bouquet of exotic, oriental spice borne on hot desert wind.

An unspoken direction: Matty pulled aside the hessian and knew precisely where to look. The knot of the handkerchief, a makeshift parcel, peeked from between the flaps of the torn shirt, its buttons doubtless ripped away when the villagers set to work on Altair. Matty pressed his mutilated palms together over the loose knot, a semblance of prayer, and grasped the blood-soaked bundle.

Pain pulsed in his hands and he welcomed it. It had purpose, was a form of energy – a promise of the power to come. The bundle shivered. He rose from his strange obeisance and turned to the millstones and its winged guardian.

The eagle squawked again, in anticipation, and Matty found himself smiling for the first time in an age.

He stood before the eagle and extended his offering. He knew now. Body parts of children, cruelly torn away by men or their machines and discarded to rot away. They had value when reunited with their maimed owners. When their owners offered them to powers older and wiser.

"You understand, Matty. It is all grist to his mill. I offered my tongue, and still I speak. Give him your fingers, and you will find your hands are not idle."

The eagle dipped its head and pecked at the bundle. The knot fell away, and the handkerchief opened. Matty adjusted his hands, formed a makeshift cup to keep the fingers and thumbs from falling to the floor. The scimitar beak took each one gently, its steel nuzzling Matty's maimed hands. It felt like sparks of electricity in his hands.

And Matty knew the name of the eagle now. "Aquila," he whispered, and tears of joy filled his eyes. He knew the answer to Altair's father's riddle as well.

Where does night begin? It begins in the heavens, when the constellation Aquila loses its brightest star, Altair. It ends not with a mere earthly dawn, but with the reclamation of the stellar light by its father.

"Yes, Nefelibata. You understand now, my brother."

His vision blurred, he nonetheless saw the night end. Saw the twin lights in its eyes that burned with cosmic fury as the eagle extended its wings to their full span, the pinions brushing the opposing walls of the windmill tower. Curtains of shimmering gold, ready to close upon the night.

This must be how angels appear, Matty thought, as the wings swept over his bowed head. But they did not embrace him; their lower feathers cleared his head as the pinions met, then parted, and the wings swept back. Again.

An angel? That is for debate.

And again, and again, faster, stronger. Dust on the mill's floor rolled in grey sheets and clumps toward the walls, as if seeking escape. The moon beams became weak intermissions between each sweep and beat of Aquila's wings, a heavenly body's gleam unable to compete with the celestial blaze of the eagle from the stars.

And with the light, the wind. A pulsing, rhythmic breeze that became a storm, a hurricane birthed in the belly of the windmill.

Matty was swept up in it, taken by it; he was lifted from the floor. There was pain in his shoulders, as harsh as the agony that struck him when he lost his hands to the machine, but this he welcomed – the eagle's talons were not gripping his flesh to destroy him, but to elevate him.

He ascended, spinning; the eagle spiralled around the upright shaft. Its blazing wings scorched the grain hoppers and the wood blackened, smoked, ignited. Fire below him, and the heavens above him.

The eagle's wings scraped the tapering walls, its pinions striking sparks against the masonry as the mill cap came closer.

The machinery gleamed in the celestial light. The brake wheel and the wallower, the crown wheel and the pinion wheel, all the machinery that harnessed the power of the wind and turned the sails to produce food – their cogs were teeth, turned a brilliant white gold in the eagle's flight.

His ascent halted here. He realised now he would not ascend to the stars. This did not sadden him; he knew Altair belonged there, not he. Altair had called him brother, but he would not take a place alongside him in the heavens.

The wind is trapped within the mill. It needs to be freed...

Another offering required. A final, terrible request, but one he acquiesced to gladly.

I'll show you what sabotage truly is, Mr Dawkins! A wooden clog is nothing compared to what a small boy's body can do... perhaps the schoolmaster would appreciate the irony before he and the Board of Guardians were consumed.

For in one of Mr Dawkins's lessons, a tale from classical times, Aquila went by another name but he was still the eagle that carried the lightning bolts of Zeus.

Divine destruction, and he, Matty Benshaw, had been honoured with a small role in this.

Aquila sensed his agreement. The claws loosened, and the meat of Matty's shoulders slid free from the talons, which transferred their grip to the horizontal wooden post of the wind shaft. The screech that followed was a cry of protest from the long-stilled machinery or one of triumph from Aquila. Perhaps both.

Matty fell into the shining teeth of the wallower and brake wheel which bit deeply.

His hands tasted fresh pain, reminding him of the agony he experienced at the teeth of the relentless, uncaring machines in the cotton mill. But this machinery welcomed the offering, thanked him for the flesh it chewed and swallowed, praising him for the blood that ran in hot rivers down the drive shaft.

Bones in both arms cracked and splintered, the wasted muscle beneath its grey-white coating of skin flensed and consumed. And still the metal teeth ground, unhindered, Matty Benshaw no obstacle to their progress but rather a lubricating grease that smoothed their turning and sped the revolutions of the wind shaft.

The hurricane shook the mill. The cap blasted into pieces with Aquila's ascension, the night sky turned into sudden daylight with its celestial blaze. And in a blink of his eye, the golden eagle was gone.

Spattered with his blood and gobbets of Matty's flesh,

the windmill sails spun rapidly. Matty could not make out the individual vanes. A hurricane in wood and canvas, spilling its rage across the headland and the institute which caused such misery and destruction.

He saw the first of the hated chimneys sway, the red brickwork at its base crumbling and then exploding.

He did not see the tower fall into the workhouse and the industrial complex, but knew from its direction the treadmill chamber would be the first to be destroyed.

That image he kept in his mind as the crown wheel's teeth bit into his skull and fed on his inner being, and he became fully one with the machine and the elemental forces that powered it.

And in the night sky, the constellation Aquila burned as fiercely as the retributive infernos that took hold of the mill and the orphanage.

None more brightly than the star Altair.

Dull Den

By Allen Ashley

This is how your life goes: you study hard at school and get into a half-decent university, coming out with a degree of independence and drive. You take a couple of starter jobs before settling into a proper career. You surround yourself with acquisitions. It should get easier but it gets harder. You work longer and longer hours just to get the endless succession of tasks done. Then you find yourself on the other side of a couple of messy but comparatively inexpensive divorces, still toiling away at your chosen profession. But now you're in your forties and your boss wants to employ young bucks who show drive and enthusiasm and an energy that has been drained from you over the past few years. And who never ask awkward questions. Still, you're senior or at least middle management – you think – so you ought to be able to survive the current cull.

Mr Diablo. My erstwhile employer; now my sworn enemy. I'm about fifty percent of the way towards bringing him crashing down. No more guest appearances on the '*Dragon's Den* Christmas Special', no more opinion columns in the *Daily Mail*. No more bankrolling puppet local councillors.

I try to hold onto the maxim that revenge is a dish best served cold. But it feels like I've taken yesterday's leftovers out of the fridge because I can't be arsed to cook anything new and fresh.

The redundancy settlement was less than generous.

"You've got transferable skills, Martin," he said to me. "You'll walk into a new job."

I didn't want a new job. For all its drawbacks, and the unsavoury aspects I didn't yet feel able to talk about, I still wanted to hold onto what I had. It made no sense to let me go – I was doing the work of three people and, besides, there's no substitute for experience. And knowledge. Ah, that was my downfall. I had stumbled upon something stronger than the usual grey areas of items claimed back against tax. I had found that Diablo was running a shadow business that didn't register with Companies House, HMRC, the Vatman or anybody else who might be interested. My revelations could potentially bring him and his business empire crashing down. I didn't have absolute proof yet but I had some leads to follow up.

Rather than spend my time in a more positive manner,

carving out a new career with a socially conscious employer.

***

Never talk to strangers in pubs. Even those who have contacted you directly via the internet. You can't be sure where it's going to lead.

OK, I admit, it got me some cash in hand work once with a removals firm in the pleasant company of a local sort known as 'Eric' but, in general, what's spoken of in *The Star and Garter* should stay there.

In his email, he'd called himself 'A. Friend' along with the enticing header: *Martin, I can help you with your redundancy and other issues*. In real life, he called himself 'Sir Terence', although his mates who came and went with alarming frequency simply referred to him as 'Cert'. As in 'Dead Cert'...?

I couldn't work out whether he was running a sophisticated drugs ring in which no money or gear ever actually changed hands or if he was just a popular chap who'd moved himself down into what I'd naively thought of as my manor.

Terence – 'Cert', oh I got it now, 'Sir T' – batted away most of my questions whilst insisting that he definitely could and would help me. "I'm not the brains or the brawn or even the mouthpiece behind this organisation," he stated between his fifth and sixth pint of Stella. "The true guiding light is young Den over there." He gesticulated vaguely at a somewhat unkempt character pumping 20p coins into a fruit machine.

"So what is your role?" I slurred.

"I suppose...I'm the interpreter. Yeah, that sums it up nicely."

If he revealed anything else, I didn't hear it as Den began making a commotion about three oranges and why wasn't the 'nudge' bar working properly. He began pounding the glass screen, yelling, "Death to machines!" before the tattooed barman walked round the counter to remove him from the premises with the classic *EastEnders* quoting line of: "You're barred, son. And your mates."

***

The trip to Pakistan had been a game-changer. I had known conditions there would be deemed unacceptable by European Union standards but nothing had prepared me for the squalor and the diabolical working conditions that I encountered on the inside of our subsidiary operation. Low wattage light bulbs swinging on loose flexes; street children with bare feet crouched into dark corners sewing the distinctive stitching for our high-brand trainers. How did they even manage to see what they were doing? Where did they eat, sleep, urinate? When did their shifts end...ever?

"Got to keep costs down to compete with those clowns at Nike and Puma," Mr Diablo beamed. "No one around here employs adults. Except for one overseer."

This official was a corpulent guy with a yard broom moustache and an odour of liberally sprinkled cheap cologne. That was the only liberal thing about him. He spent most of our visit either bowing obsequiously to 'the master' or fiddling with his black leather belt, untying it a couple of times as a warning to recalcitrant employees.

Of course, we were aware of terrorism and security issues. Diablo kept up a sunbed perma-tan but with my ginger hair and lightly freckled complexion I stood out as undeniably Celtic. We sped around the rough and not so rough but still overcrowded areas in an old black Roller that had the same number plate as his Audi at home – dee one four bee ell oh – which I thought would be illegal in this globalised world. Diablo had no children, just a couple of feckless public school nephews. I had lately begun to suspect that he was grooming me – not in the internet paedophile sense! – to take over. I had begun to suspect that I wasn't really up to it and, in fact, would rather look for a more socially responsible job doing something worthwhile for the community. Those thoughts hadn't crystallised but the conditions that I saw in Pakistan made my mind up to leave his employ. When I could face telling him. When I had an alternative.

"Efficiency, Martin, that's the key. We need an operation

like this in England. Maybe a couple."

"Workers might not...relish such conditions, Mr Diablo."

"It's a brave new world, son. The trade unions are dead. People will put up with a lot more in order to hold onto their jobs."

The second factory was worse than the first. Dirty machines, sweating workers, incessant noise, the combined aromas of grease, oil, burnt rice, tanned leather, perspiration and other bodily expellants. In the dimness, the child labourers seemed to be literally tied to their posts by the pendulous cables carrying low-wattage light bulbs across the ceiling. Their dirty, bare feet – no free trainers or other perks for those actually producing the goods – appeared to have taken scrubby root in the cluttered shop floor. Their nimble hands moved like oversized tree-dwelling insects in a warped forest of hateful machinery. I was from solid working class stock and the so-called benefits of Victorian industrialisation and expansion had likely done nothing to improve the lives of my ancestors. Likewise the Empire. Which had perhaps never gone away: instead, it was characterised nowadays by a rich British businessman still finding ways to exploit the urchins of the Indian sub-continent.

On the plane home, Diablo commandeered the window seat so that all I could see was the occasional white cloud supporting our jumbo's weight. The film was a desperately predictable rom-com. The in-flight magazine carried an article about the future of space exploration involving cyborgs – augmented, part-robot humans adapted to deal with and survive the troubling conditions. Where should we draw the line between who or what is fully human and where does that definition end?

"Make my day, punk," Diablo misquoted, reading over my shoulder.

That was months ago yet there hadn't been a single day or uncomfortable night since when I had been able to put my experiences out of my mind. Then I had discovered the hidden folder: subtly siphoned-off profits, blueprints for a building on an out of town industrial estate, plans to bring the heinous practices to Britain and to further push the boundaries of acceptable industrial conditions. Playing on the needs of the desperate amidst the public service cuts, the continuing austerity, the tricks the government used to change benefit eligibility rules and that prevailing capitalist requirement to produce.

All I needed to spring into action was the address of this new factory. But somehow he must have got wind of my intentions because I was suddenly surplus to requirements. Out on my ear. But, mixing metaphors like a bad sixth form poet, still with a fire in my belly. Den and the Dullards might yet be my salvation.

***

In truth, I didn't expect to see the two young bucks again but the very next morning they were lurking outside the newly refurbished Jobcentre Plus building.

"Don't waste your time going in there, Martin. We can help you do what you want to do. Come on."

Just how much had I told them last night?

I followed them to a nondescript black Mazda. Den went to open the driver's door but Terence pushed him out of the way.

"He had a bit of an accident with a bit of a TWOC a while back," he explained. "He used to be the brightest tool in the box but now...sometimes he can be a bit dull Den. You wanna ride shotgun?"

"Not if there are any actual shotguns."

Neither man reacted so I opened the passenger side and made myself comfortable.

"Do your belt up, mate," Terence ordered.

"I thought you guys were...outlaws...gangsters...whatever the word is these days."

"We are; but the dashboard bleeps like a fucker if you don't belt up. Does my nut in."

As we headed out of town I began to wonder whether I should have taken a literal back seat as Den behind me kept up a constant barrage of anti-mechanistic oration and threats to incapacitate any machine he could get his hands on. You'd have been forgiven for thinking his parents got shot by Daleks. Watching the shabby grey buildings fade and the scrubby brown fields take their place, I constantly wondered where our philosopher would choose to draw the line. Should we even have been travelling in a motorised vehicle; wouldn't it be truer to the cause to trot around in a horse and cart like the Amish?

"Use this," Terence instructed, one hand on the wheel, the other passing me a shrink-wrapped package which contained a white plastic face mask in the shape of 'Comedy'. Den and Terence had 'Tragedy', leaving me the clown of the trio.

A couple of other vehicles had already turned up at the factory car park. We were just in time for the shift change. Several of the other disguised protestors held neatly produced placards proclaiming our cause. I joined in as best I could.

The starring role, however, was taken by Den. On previous evidence, I'd had him down as being somewhere on the autistic spectrum but he came into his own on this occasion as he pranced around in front of the downcast workers and berated their life choices.

"Wage slaves! Factory clones! Wasting your existence in subservience to Mammon. Clock off now and don't ever come back. Reclaim your existence while you can."

Many of the people he intercepted simply shook their head and shrugged at his proclamations. It took me several minutes to deduce that they were probably Eastern European immigrants shipped over here as cheaper labour; the intricacies of English pastoral rhetoric were lost on them.

They were just honest folk trying to earn a living for themselves and their family. The real enemies were the bosses and owners. But they were nowhere to be seen. Not even bothering to use their i-phones to call the cops on us.

The demonstration died down, fizzling to near-extinction like a spent firecracker. Den, though, was still pumped up and in the mood to destroy.

"We'll take a little detour on the way back," Terence promised.

After ten aimless minutes hurtling along country lanes we spotted a phone booth at the edge of a nondescript village green. I opened the door and immediately gagged at the smell of dog shit and fertiliser. Den was off towards the target with his trusty sledgehammer. I pulled my jacket up to break the gag reflex. Terence let the younger guy have his way for a few minutes before calling him back. Even though I was a bystander, I felt that suddenly I had achieved a rapport with these new acquaintances and was reliving my misspent youth. That I hadn't actually misspent. I sneaked a look at my mobile but was getting no reception. That public call box – a rare enough sight these days – was probably somebody's lifeline in the past and maybe again in the future. Our vandalism seemed pointless. Like vandalism had ever been logical...

"No coins. It don't take no coins," Den muttered, returning. "Credit cards only. More imprisonment to the great controlling machine."

I spent our return journey marvelling that he could actually read. I got them to drop me off a few streets from my flat, just in case GPS or CCTV was onto us.

***

Diablo was on the regional news having made some minor donation of a few pairs of trainers to a local school's sports club. Since they exposed Jimmy Savile, no-one is ever going to be fooled again by public good deeds masking private crimes and misdemeanours. At least, that's my hope.

I continued to worry that the little guy or little guys could no longer so easily bring down the bigger players. As for our anarchist sect, the self-styled Den and the Dullards, what a ragtag bunch we were: me, an unemployed operations manager with a grudge and a newly-grown conscience; Den, an idiot savant intent on destroying machines; Terence, his manipulative minder with a tendency towards sudden violence; Spinning Jenny, a talented, subtly attractive female who liked hanging around the bad boys; plus various other hangers-on and foot soldiers with monikers like Oxy Moron and Key Smith. I couldn't imagine that Nike or Adidas would be quaking in their designer boots. But Diablo Sports and Leisure...

Maybe this wasn't even really about him and his hateful

company. Maybe it was mostly about me and my needs. I could still withdraw, leave these small-time revolutionaries to their nocturnal destruction and instead set about rebuilding my life. Maybe volunteer somewhere once or twice a week – a charity shop, an animal shelter – whilst I waited for my next job. Maybe download a dating app or join a creative class at my local church or library…the possibilities were limitless.

The choice had already been made. Once the express train is on the track its course is set. No time to pause or backtrack. Death to Diablo's infernal machines!

***

We pulled up in two vans and one removals lorry at an industrial estate some twenty minutes out of town. These places with their locked barriers and Gestapo searchlights, coupled with a sense of human desertion yet lingering presence of evil, always gave me the creeps. There was no time to waste, though. Sir Terence handed out strips of aluminium foil out of which we fashioned CCTV-confusing headgear. Spinning Jenny was handy as ever with the bolt cutters and then, like cockroaches scrabbling into the food cupboard, we were in and across the car park, heading for the main buildings.

"Death to machines!" Dull Den roared before Sirt's grimy hand shushed him.

Every time I went anywhere near a factory I had the shakes and memories to overcome. I even got the tremors simply watching a BBC News item about downturns or upturns in industrial output. What I'd seen in Pakistan had shocked and scarred me. Kids, young people, harnessed into position for greater efficiency, each finger linked to a function like a child prodigy in a warped prog-rock band; clothed only in a diaper so that the four-hour or six-hour or twelve-hour shifts need not be interrupted by any calls of nature. Only when the worker was ready to drop from total exhaustion would the higher caste foreman give the instructions for the harnesses to be relaxed and the 'operative' to be released; with an industrious replacement ready and, apparently, willing to step into the breach.

"Jackpot!" Sirt was yelling. "Hey, get over here! Oxy, Oxy!"

Lathes were his particular taste. He and his crew set about 'liberating' this specimen from its coupling to the factory floor with their oxy-acetylene torches. I headed for the overseer's office, switching on computers and trying the usual simplistic log-in codes that ninety percent of companies thought were sufficient to protect their vital data. I also began pulling out paper files, looking for incriminating evidence of illegal practices, tax dodges, health and safety breaches.

Half an hour was the time we'd allowed ourselves and it yielded some little treasure. Sure, the modern machine wreckers of the Dullards had bypassed the local alarm system but we couldn't afford to get sloppy or over-confident. I returned to the shop floor where another of the troops – Oxy Tone, I think it was – had just loaded another potentially valuable modern artefact onto the back of a lorry. Ready to sell on the black market at about a tenth of what it was actually worth.

"From fuck this to fork-lift to full mitts," was Terence's succinct summation of the process.

In fact, Sir T was looking well-satisfied with his night's work but Den was stood with sledgehammer swinging menacingly from hand-to-hand like a constipated caveman. He was vaguely humming a nursery rhyme to himself. Despite my best efforts at innocent non-involvement, he somehow caught my eye.

"Wanna smash machines," he muttered.

"And you will, Den, you will," Terence stated, gently guiding him by the shoulder towards a darkened corner.

I followed discreetly. Sir T, who possessed an enviable knack for rapidly assessing the layout of all new locations, flicked on the overhead lights, revealing a large contraption for weighing packages. It was the sort of thing they still used in the freight area of the larger railway stations. I couldn't quite work out why Den would want to vent his ire on this contraption unless he was annoyed that a new fad diet wasn't helping him to shift the pounds. Still, when Terence invited him to do his worst, Den set about the smash-up job with gusto.

"You killed my dad," he yelled. "You killed me," he

added in a bizarre non-sequitur.

When the noise grew too bad, I headed back to the van where Spinning Jenny had the radio tuned to the police frequency as a necessary precaution.

Since the first mission she'd taken something of a shine to me.

"Can I have one back-up vehicle, please, and a paramedic to attend a collision on Copeland Street?"

Beneath the grime and the boyish attire of jeans and polo shirt, she was quite attractive in an elfin sort of way.

"Domestic at Rawnsley Estate. One male in custody. I need a WPC here to attend to attend to young female participant."

We indulged in some slow snogging and a bit of tit touching before a sharp tap on the passenger side window halted our amorous activities.

"Laters, Martin," she whispered, as Den and Terence clambered in and we screeched away towards the anonymity of the closest 'A' road.

***

It was three days later when I caught up with the gang again, calm and unruffled and above the law back in their favourite boozer. Sir Terence was chucking peanuts into an ashtray – what pubs even kept ashtrays anymore? – and Den was at the no-armed bandit nudging his way to a minor win. Complete with Spinning Jenny hanging onto his leather-jacketed arm. She didn't even raise an eyebrow when I walked past her on the way back from the gents.

"Hey, Martin," Terence offered, "that was some fine work the other night. I sold on loads of that gear. Here's a couple of hundred for your trouble."

My hand hesitated. Taking the cash would be yet another confirmation of my entanglement in their illegal activities. But redundancy pay-offs don't last forever. I pocketed the bundle.

"That still wasn't the place I'm looking for," I answered.

"Come and ride with us again one night. We'll find that hellhole. Hey, won't we, Den?" he called, suddenly loud and refocused.

No response. "Den? What about the machines, what have they done to you?"

The younger man's response was inaudible. I waited awkwardly, not sure whether this was to be another long night set putting the legal world to rights. "I've been meaning to ask you something," I began. "You and Den? You seem...an odd mix. Just wondering but: why do you hang around together so much?"

"He's my brother, that's all. Not metaphorical, like, but actual, blood-flesh. 'S it got to do with you, office clone?"

"Absolutely nothing."

"That's right. Now while you're so flush with the cash,

get us another round in. And buy yourself some nuts. I think you dropped the last lot."

I passed the odd couple on the way to the bar. Den was a couple of nudges away from a four in a row payout. He was mumbling constantly to himself. I could only pick out the occasional word or strangled syllable but they seemed to be from his regular anti-mechanistic spiel. Sniffing the proximity of jackpot loot, Jenny nuzzled in closer to his left shoulder. "You're a poet, you are," she cooed.

I managed one bitter shandy before I made my excuses and left them all to it.

***

As I walked back home, I was bumped into by someone too busy manipulating the functions of their phone to pay any attention to their physical progress.

"You're lucky I'm a pedestrian not a car," I called to their departing back, "you'd be dead by now."

"You're dead already, pal," he retorted.

Then I went into a gloomy despond of how in our modern, so-called civilised world we've become over-reliant on our machines and devices. You're not even alive if you're not all over Facebook, Twitter, Instagram, Snapchat and all that shit. Most money is just electronic transfers – data, basically.

Eat natural and buy an apple that's been picked by a machine, packed on a production line, driven in a lorry, unloaded on a fork-lift.

The doctors are keeping us in our vegetable existence with their high-tech life-support systems. Are you sure we are truly alive?

***

I had got into the habit of checking my bank balance online every day, waiting for the second half of my redundancy settlement to appear magically via bank transfer. Which it had yet to do.

I could put if off no longer and had to call Diablo Sports and Leisure Wear to make enquiries. I got through to Caroline, PA to the chief executive. Diablo had spent most of the past two years trying to persuade her 'away from her lesbian tendencies' and into his bed. Or highly polished desk top. Such office politicking no longer bothered me; unpaid wages did.

"Oh hi, Martin, how are you going? Any work yet? No? Oh well, something will crop up. The boss is…out on a visit at the moment. Shall I pass on your best wishes?"

A day later, they made a payment into my current account. It was welcome, of course, but still a few hundred pounds short of what I was owed. I got the impression that this was the final transaction.

I had read somewhere that most successful bands split up over royalty issues. The back pages of the tabloids were full of footballers looking for huge signing-on fees or angling for a transfer because a team mate or international colleague was on better wages. The history books implied that many wars from as far back as England claiming parts of France, probably even as remote as Roman times, were essentially fought over money or its previous incarnations of gold and salt.

As if I needed any further motivation. Let's add to that hateful list.

***

There was a back room in one of the Pakistan factories that took my breath away. And not simply as a gagging reflex against the unwashed flesh, the hot machines and the regurgitated air. This was a part that I was not supposed to enter but Diablo and the overseer had absented themselves to talk output figures over a pot of tea in the barely habitable head office; so I had started to wander. My smart suit and my Caucasian skin would offer me both protection and access.

There was one workshop where a brown-skinned kid in a dhoti was moving his fingers so swiftly that they became a blur. When I blinked, I ascertained that there was no clear divisor between his digits and the incessant back and forth motion of the machine we called the stitcher. I looked at his bare feet and they had melded into the metal base as if everything had at one stage been heated, melted, and then cooled down into a combined structure. In fact, every part of him was permanently fused into the machinery. This would be the shift that never ended until all flesh had worn away. This was death on the job – if he could be adequately described as still living. I thought I detected a faint quiver around the lips and some slight expansion and contraction around the chest area. But his eyes were gone to vacancy. And it was that more than anything else that stopped me looking for a pickaxe or a shovel or some other tool with which to extricate this tiny homo sapiens from the gross mechanism.

I backed out of the room, closed the door. I'm not proud of my inaction. But I own it.

***

We had taken to somewhat aimlessly patrolling the ring road in Terence's black Mazda looking for unsigned exits that might lead to secret factories. Terence assured me that Den had experienced a premonition, that we would be lucky very soon. The scruff seemed so far out of the present tense most of the time that the notion of him receiving intimations of future fate was laughable. And yet…maybe he had been blessed by a badly-tattooed Lady Luck on her last trip to Lidl.

"Hang on," I yelled, "that's his car!"

"Hey? Who, Simon Cowell?"

"Worse than that. Look at that number plate – dee one four bee ell oh."

"Right, Martin, I'm on it. Not too obvious, eh? Let's see where that Rolls Royce is headed. Nice car; bugger to hot-wire, though."

As unobtrusively as possible, we settled into Diablo's vehicular slipstream. After six minutes, his smooth suspension took him off at a slip road that we almost missed. Our screeching brakes and sudden swerve should have alerted him to our predatory presence. Maybe his blasé confidence was shielding him from everything, as usual.

Diablo parked by a grey, blocky building like something out of a Stalinist textbook. We motored on for a couple of hundred yards, pulled onto the verge, pondered.

"That's got to be the place."

"OK, Martin, I'm with you. Hey, Den, we're on a mission, kid. Could be up to some smashing tonight."

"Death to machines!" he mumbled from the back seat, face partially hidden by a zipped hoodie.

Sir Terence had some apps that enabled him to pass on the news and round up a mob in quick time. They would be locking on to some sort of military level GPS signal that he'd acquired from a disillusioned veteran from the Afghanistan conflict. For good measure, he got me to update Den's Facebook page with a cryptic message. Whilst we waited for back-up to arrive, we all stepped out of the car and found a tree to urinate against ahead of our destructive and vengeful mission. Once again, I wondered about the technical capability of this anti-industrialist army, knowingly employing social media and technology to try to take us back to pastoral bliss.

A small convoy of discontinued car brands, beaten-up vans and a decommissioned ambulance passed us in slow procession. Before you could count to five hundred every one of them had performed a U-turn and parked up. We busied ourselves acquiring masks, weapons and spray paint. I stopped for only a moment to think about how quickly I had gone from being a sales executive in an Italian suit to a fully-fledged member of the underclass. Maybe this was how all revolutions started, with a snowball effect that took the law-abiding citizens onto a crash course in direct action.

"Let's do this!" Sirt stated.

"Any...uh, plan of action?" I asked.

"Go with the flow, feller. Let it come naturally."

"Back to nature," Dull Den muttered, exiting the back passenger seat.

I felt like I'd been cast into one of those films about football hooliganism that had been so popular some years back. I half-expected us to break into a team chant at any second. Sir Terence, though, was out at the front urging a quiet, covert approach.

The factory doors weren't even locked.

Maybe they thought no-one would ever bother them out here on the by-road to nowhere.

Maybe they were half-expecting us.

We entered to noise and heat. I had thought that we had assembled a sizeable rag-tag army but we were faced with the TARDIS effect of the building appearing much bigger on the inside and at every yard or so an assembly station or a fitting and fixing area and each one was occupied. There must have been thousands of people working there. Diablo's secret operation was even greater than I'd suspected or feared.

Den stepped to the front of our advance, wiped a bead of sweat off his grimy forehead and proclaimed above the din, "Arise brothers and sisters! Throw off your shackles and leave with us."

He projected his message with a voice that one might have described as surprisingly stentorian. Those on the upper floors would have struggled to hear him but the closer workers seemed to be paying attention. A hit squad from our party had already detached itself in search of the power switches and they struck lucky early doors. The assembly line in front of us came to a juddering halt. A few of the factory clones disentangled themselves, got groggily to their feet, swayed from one leg to the other like unfocused zombies. Scanning the rest of the visible area, though, I could see that many of the operatives were lashed in to their stations; some seemed to have fully melded into cost-effective, stationary cyborgs. Freedom for all might be a harder goal to achieve than we'd anticipated. Where did flesh end and metal or plastic start?

We were suddenly plunged into darkness as one of our crew flicked the mains switch. Emergency lighting kicked in after a few seconds, bathing the scene in an appropriately dim reddish glow.

"Death to machines!"

I held back slightly, feeling that the fusion had gone so far that destroying some of these machines would mean murdering their human conjunctions, too. This was the future of the industrial process and, sure, I wanted no part of it but at base I was a peaceful man. Live and let –

A spanner hit me in the arm. Thrown by some jumped-up supervisor in that direction. Bastard. I'll have him.

Maybe I did, maybe I didn't. Den and Sir Terence had led the charge onto the shop floor but I realised that the modern history books had it right: in the midst of every battle reigned only confusion. Protect your own face; lash out at your enemy when you can. Clang, crash, metallic scraping like jumbo jets taxiing onto the same runway. The factory floor, lit in weak russet illumination, was like a war in hell. I held my own position, not really advancing, wary glances cast all around, trying to track the progress of the battle. Someone on the industry side had restored one of the generators but the machines were running out of sync, goods backing up, conveyor belts buckling as our crew took the hand-to-hand fight onto their rolling tread. Details became lost in the chaos of sound and fury.

I saw some limbs lost to whirling blades, joints crushed by sledgehammer blows. The screams were human and yet their pitch was like the whistle calling us all onto shift.

What was I doing here with this dodgiest of crowds led by the mad machine-wrecker Dull Den and the manipulative miser Sir Terence? I should absent myself whilst I still could. This wasn't really my fight. And yet I was culpable in bringing them here to this scene of Armageddon.

I could smell machine oil; then that was supplanted by fire and smoke as the gears ground against each other and sparked flames to go with the redness of the strip lights. I thought I caught a glimpse of my hateful old boss Diablo, his newly grown pointed beard and hideous grin leering from the top of the stairs. I tried to give chase but my legs wouldn't move. I glanced down and saw that I was chained into place. How had that happened?

Spinning Jenny had fallen close by. I could have taken a tissue out of my pocket, waved it like the international symbol for mercy, administered First Aid to her prone form. But I didn't. Instead, I grabbed at the axe her supine hand had let fall. I twisted with exertion, chopping at the chains around my feet. But the blade went right through; it simply didn't connect and ricocheted off the stone floor. Still, I kept up my axe attack.

These chains were real yet not tangible.

That didn't mean I should stop. No, it was my task to chop away, to free the working man and woman from the centuries of industrialised drudgery, of wage slavery, of appalling conditions, of flouting of health and safety, strike a blow now, and again now, keep cutting at the chains, the chains of de-unionisation, of managers and corporate bosses ruling and ruining lives, of blasé restructurings, of increased hours for worse pay, of profit margins for the shareholders only, of squeezing the workforce in a vice of fear and necessity, strike at those chains, come on, the chains of no other future being conceivable, of the morning hooter and the clocking-in card, of seven days a week of toil, of twenty-four hours of toil, of the merging of man and machine into the dehumanising efficiency that's required by the profit margin, *their* profit margin, no choice but to be bound to their vision of progress, keep fighting back, come on, chop away... until at last one link is broken...and then another...and another.

The black Mazda is a machine that will transport me home where I can watch the information machine screens to see what really happened or what they are prepared to admit happened and then I'm at the cash point machine withdrawing all I have, notes tangible in my hand, machine-crafted, offering me options that all come down to options moulded by two hundred or more years of industrialisation, no going back, this is the world as we know it today.

No going back to hell-hole factory, office drudgery, wage slavery. I shall live on the margins full-time now. Dull Den may be lost in the latest battle but I can pick up the mantle, carry on his Ned Ludd cause.

It's what will keep me human.

March of the Midnight Crow

By Leah Crowley

The night sky closed in. The moon shivered cold, flickering light shimmered upon wolves prowling the marsh.

Edenhurst Village. A population of one hundred poverty-stricken families. It was late. Children were read bedtime stories. Fathers transformed from their evening wear into protective attire, readying themselves for the March. Each wore something damned, stitched with innocent memories of the Dead.

Days of endless mourning were only an imaginary dream.

Smoked ash from burnt out buildings rose from cobble-stoned ground. Once the plague had taken hold, everything had, everything *needed* to burn. Nothing diseased could remain. All traces of humanity expunged. Immortality was their only hope in saying goodbye to the dreaded Curse – that was what the priest called it – everybody else knew different even if they didn't dare speak of it.

Dominic and his family – two daughters and a son – were descended from good Roman Catholic stock. They had the strictest of upbringings. Every morning they would attend their parish church at five o'clock, thoroughly washed and dressed in their sartorial religious garb, never leaving home without Bible in hand – their protective cleansing from mental discouragement was to have the Good Book with them at all times. Disobeying their father was one thing, but to disobey the Holy Father would lead to vicious consequences...their family, children included, worshipped the incumbent pope, Clement VI, almost to a fault.

Outside in the courtyard was the sound of squealing pigs, the clucks of chickens on the loose, as they all snuffled amongst the stale and infested garbage from the day's now forgotten residents.

Dominic headed into his bedroom: basic - a thin mattress resting on an iron frame, lying in the centre of this small boxed room. Displayed above the bed was a larger than life pictorial representation of God; either side sat two small chests of drawers, filled with identical robes. Against the wall, a plain wooden closet. He felt incredibly blessed to don his overtly powerful crow-like mask and associated garments. They were the only items stored in his closet. The fragranced scents of lemon and mint wafted throughout the house. The ingredients a necessity for the protection against the miasmatic polluted air.

He would admit that he felt fear the first time he wore his doctor's outfit; the crow-like beak of the mask was a frightening method to inflict a thorough examination of the Cursed victims, without actually touching them. Because of his prestigious role, he was an isolated man, unable to interact fully with society.

After all, to do so could mean the contagious virus might spread even further...

***

Tonight would be hectic – Dominic was to draw a vast amount of blood from a family of five. They had already been quarantined and forbidden from leaving their dwelling. He was upset – not because of the task ahead but because of his youngest daughter, Helena, was unwell with a rare and horrific pox. He knew she was living on borrowed time – only six years old; she should have had so many years left – was this God's punishment because of his work with the Curse?

He walked into Helena's room. There she lay, within her own sodden sheets, so weakened by disease, but her empty innocent face portrayed a reflective moment. Rapturous lucidity. His heart raced like anguished lightning, witnessing his beloved daughter like this, defenceless to the world, it was breaking him.

"Daughter, I soon must leave. Another family requires healing. Remember I love you with all my heart. Pope Clement and the other Holy Fathers will protect you in my absence," he whispered.

"Please don't go!" Helena called.

"I must. It is important I heal this other family." Dominic was becoming emotional – he didn't know if when he returned he would be informed of his daughter's departing. It was a strong possibility. He wiped a tear from his emotion-stricken face and headed back to his room to finish preparations. There was only thirty minutes before his blood-letting task was to begin.

He opened his closet. Such visions of sadness, of despair, impaired his thoughts. The terrifying-looking beak shaped mask, made from tough leather, hung above his other mysterious garments.

Remembering he had to refill the beak - which had an opening for the required scented chemicals - he went downstairs to fetch vinegar and sweet oiled ingredients. These were used to hide the stench of death of those corpses which were unburied.

As he went into the pantry to retrieve the needed items, he heard his daughter's painful cries. He hoped his other daughter, Ruth, who had been silently sleeping, would not waken due to her sister's cacophony.

***

It was the dead of night, soon perhaps to be the deadliest.

Last week Dominic had been told this dreaded Curse had infected and destroyed more than two thousand living souls. When Pope Clement heard this news, he shrugged and damned the whole of Edenhurst village, including the surrounding populated vicinities. Nobody was to be spared – that was his edict.

Dominic headed back to his room; in his arms he held the tray of concocted remedies. There was a sudden commotion from inside the closet. He opened the door with one hand; with the other he placed the tray of bottled ingredients on the bed.

Lying there on the floor, crimson piercing glass eyepieces, standing out from their metal frames, looked up at him. They had the stare of a carnal hunting bird with a thirst for blood – yet these were supposedly insusceptible to this evil plague.

In front of him hung his black overcoat and the other garments of protection. He turned his head away slightly, his nose was overpowered with a stale suet odour; the strong residue had been rubbed into his costume to protect him from a possible risk of disease from the suffering population. He didn't know how affective it had been.

He pressed on. Dominic grabbed his leather breeches and stepped into them. He placed the waxed-canvas gown over his head and securely tightened it under his armpits, around his neck and waist. He gazed at the crow-like mask for a moment of clarity, placed it upon his trembling face.

Dominic picked up the red-eyed glasses and secured them to his nose. He fetched the dark overcoat and wrapped it around his shoulders, gently fastening the buttons. He put on his leather hat and soft gloves. He stared in the mirror, located at the side of the closet; his religious life faded into another world, his reflection now was a healing masquerade.

A wooden cuckoo-clock chimed loud from the hallway; the time of judgement was almost upon him. Dominic looked once more into the mirror with his wooden cane in hand - the cane was tucked and fastened onto his waist belt at the end of most practices. He hoped tonight's would be no exception. It was there for his protection.

Ravens could be heard from the woodland, crying out for a nocturnal salvation. Many villagers said that these birds were a blessing from the diseased souls.

Dominic swung his cane in rotating motions; his whole body was heavily guarded by this birdman disguise. He walked down the wooden staircase, squeaking in his leather. Traces of scented oils and herbs followed behind.

There was a knock at the door which echoed throughout the whole building.

***

A crowded sea of plague-doctors waited in the front courtyard, silent as the autumn breeze, the crackling of rustling leaves was the only sound to be heard. Fierce black ravens perched on roofs, looking mischievous, stared on.

The March had begun.

Ferocious winds attacked their dark shadowed walk.

The head priest of the village church wore a darker shade of red glasses, in case of the awkward event of decapitation in any melee which might follow.

Many of the townsmen had gathered for this eerie, solemn evening – they had a stark choice: either save their villages or suffer the drastic consequences of the Black Death. Their wives and families suffered in their way too – access had been restricted to their husbands due to the possible contagion spreading. Such a sickening fate. For a moment Dominic appeared distracted – he couldn't but help imagine his daughter and her sufferings. He wasn't sure they would be united again after this midnight march. All he could do was pray that they would.

They marched upon the echoing cobbled streets, this brigade of destruction - animals appeared from the shadows startled and panicked before returning to their safe-places. The sky shone with a flickering autumn moon, scattered grey clouds hid from the dark figures below.

Dominic and the priest arrived at the house, two loud knocks with his clenched fist shook the worn out frame.

"Answer! We are the flightless saviours from God.

Answer and you too can be saved," Dominic called.

Silence.

The troop of other mysterious doctors scattered and fluttered the wings of their blacked-out guises at other houses to check for further cursed souls. No-one would escape capture this night.

Dominic stared up at the front upper floor hatch window; a little girl stood looking down. She was afraid. He reflected about his own sick Helena, these girls could have been the same age. They looked so similar.

The priest standing next to him, cane in hand, banged fiercely upon the door, the force of which broke both hinges. The girl screamed, ran downstairs to safeguard her family from the two haunting crow-like men as they barged into her home.

In the front facing room, two unwell souls lay upon a hammock. Sweat began to suffocate the plague-doctors from their heavy protective clothes.

The girl clutched her mother close, as if she was a long, lost teddy-bear. The woman was gaunt, withered, unresponsive - murmuring sounds came with a frightened and confused pain.

Two family members already deceased; Dominic knew this from poking his wooden cane into the bodies, the girl was the only untouched survivor. The Curse had passed her by. She would be taken away into protective custody and sent to a work house to spend her remaining days. Their role, for the evening, was complete.

Dominic was ordered to be quarantined, avoiding all possibilities of spreading the decaying infection. He would never see his daughter again. When the priest told him, his expression was like a muted boy; his whole life he had strived to guide and protect his family but also to be the most caring, loving Father.

To be both, it seemed, meant a price to pay.

He headed outside, into the courtyard. Images of a faded and failed nation confronted him.

The plague-doctors gathered.

Dominic removed his mask and breathed in the air.

The night was still, etched in sadness and deployed memories of evil.

The midnight crows gazed into the blackened sky, rotating their beaks into a sequence of searching for a sombre peace...

A Prospect Greater Than The Sea

By Dean M. Drinkel

"On ne voit bien qu'avec la coeur." – Antoine de Saint-Exupéry

"Être adulte c'est être seul." – Jean Rostand

"The past is a different country, they do things differently there." – L.P. Hartley

Requiescats were chanted as the train pulled into the station. I ignored them - they weren't for me, weren't my business. Echoes in someone else's dream.

When I stepped onto the platform, I wasn't surprised or

disheartened that he wasn't there but I was disappointed.

For an hour or so I stood on the street waiting.

The sun scorched my skin.

I was alone but I wasn't lonely – I had memories of this place, I had memories of him. That was why I had travelled so far and put myself at so much risk.

It was all for him.

It always had been.

***

Obviously I tried ringing the number they'd given me and it worked first time though nobody answered. I dropped the phone back into my pocket.

Perhaps it was the sun: I was disorientated momentarily. I tried to get my bearings. I was exactly where I wanted to be, everything was familiar but there was something...*outre* about the whole thing...it was probably just me, I had been absent for a while.

I was worried that if I didn't hook up with him quickly then everything was going to be out of synch and prove that the *experiment* didn't work. I had called their bluff but if I wasn't careful I was going to be the one with egg on my face.

When initial contact had been made (not by me – that wasn't allowed), it had been agreed that I would stay with him

– now I was here however, I wasn't sure if that was a good idea – I had offered myself as a sacrificial lamb, what the hell was I thinking?

Across the street was a bar – we used to drink there, though it looked very different now. It would be the ideal place to be when he did eventually turn up.

I grabbed my suitcase.

***

Must have been the heat, but I started drinking like a fish. It had been a long time since I had drunk anything tinged with alcohol and boy, whatever this local brew was, I was necking it like there was no tomorrow (the irony of that!). At first I sat outside at one of the wooden barrels so I could watch this world pass me by. I tried the phone again but still nothing.

A point did come when I half-considered returning to the station and hanging about there but why? I was happy in the bar with my beer (or whatever it was). I couldn't say exactly how long I lasted but it was a good few hours – I had even moved inside and sat by the dartboard (remember them?) to continue the imbibing. I was more than a little tipsy when I staggered out dragging my bag behind me (I'd forgotten it had wheels!). It was early evening I could wager that just about and probably win favourably.

I had been kind in thinking that he was just running late – to be fair to him it wasn't out of character, yet there was something in my bones that reminded me today was different (that his absence was somehow purposeful). I had half-hoped that at some point he might have appeared suddenly, with a broad beaming grin, begging for forgiveness and sharing a glass like the old times.

But that never happened, so I had settled my bill and staggered out onto the street.

I was unsteady; used my suitcase to keep me upright. Was I that smashed? Standing (barely!) there, it dawned on me that I needed a place to crash either for the night or even for a couple of hours – I had to sleep off the booze.

Fatigue and exhaustion threatened to derail me. The combination of travelling such a distance – literally and metaphysically - the alcohol (and I supposed not eating anything either – I had been told not to consume food before I travelled as the whole process worked better on an empty stomach) was going to knock me over if I didn't get a grip. I was an idiot, I should have had something, even a sandwich, when I arrived – I hadn't done myself any favours. I had been told to look after myself after...well, after all that had happened (of which I don't need to constantly tell you about, surely?)

For my own sanity I had to make a firm decision or all this was going to be over before it started...a wave of sadness, of desolation, came out of nowhere and smashed into me like an errant tsunami. I was worried about him as usual and if I wasn't careful I knew that emotion would be too powerful for me to function properly and I would be completely overwhelmed.

This was not how it was supposed to be. I didn't know (or care to know) the science behind it but I had paid good money for the trip. All parties agreed he would be at the station yet he wasn't.

Something had gone wrong.

That was obvious.

I prayed he was fine.

I wondered if refunds were possible.

***

At the corner of two roads I knew there was a small hotel. I had never stayed there before (and for good reason – what a debauched history it had – particularly I recalled, an incident from twenty or so years ago when a man killed his lover...it was a bloody story and one I certainly didn't want repeated). It didn't look like it had changed in all that time either; run-down, the outside paintwork peeling and dilapidated – the sign outside suggested it was cheap and had everything needed for a good night's rest.

I decided to give it a shot.

Oh, more irony.

The night-manager showed me to my room. I hadn't needed his assistance, it was easy enough to find on my own as there were only two rooms per floor. When he said he would be kind and carry my luggage for me, what could I do to stop him? The lift wasn't in use but the gods were smiling and as I was on the third floor it wasn't that far to walk.

The room hadn't cost me too much either so I wasn't out of pocket – which was good as they hadn't given me a lot of local currency. I dropped a piece of shiny metal into his palm and politely pushed him out of the room and into the corridor – I didn't need his questions and probably didn't have answers he would understand anyway. He was smiling so I presumed he was contented.

From memory, it was possible for the sun to set quickly in this part of the world. One minute it's there, the next it's gone - as if swallowed by a vacuum so densely black that the space which remains is extremely impenetrable and if you stare into it even for a millisecond, the visions you experience...no, no, I shook my head – I wasn't going there, I wasn't a back-street shaman – this wasn't mine to conjure...before I could ready myself for relaxation I sensed a darkness encroaching my personal space. I used my phone's torch and searched the walls until I found the light-switch. I went to turn it on but...

...where was I? Who was there? Someone definitely and they were reaching, ready to drag me back to where I'd come from, but that wouldn't be fair as it was far too early...

...the deal had been I was going to spend time with him - there were ghosts which needed to be put to rest, a conversation needed completing, words needed to be traded...my heart beat fast, the adrenalin flowed and my brain – the synapses exploded – all manners of existence flashed before me – my pupils dilated, my irises became concrete gardens for dancing devils...the corona of your dying sun captivated me...*tell them about the Dervish...tell everybody before it is too late..you were born to be a messiah*...I blinked repeatedly, I had to draw my imagination in before all manners of pretentiousness rewrote his story...the hair on my arms, the back of my neck: electrically charged...I had to breathe...I had to calm...why did he do this to me? Why did he leave me? Why did he...steel cockroaches clamoured over my chest.

I flipped the switch and everything was illuminated.

If there had been anybody in the room, they were gone.

I blamed my relapse on my empty stomach and beer-addled brain.

Checking that the door was locked, I collapsed onto the bed. I needed rest. Badly. This nonsense couldn't continue. My eyes were heavy...within moments I was gone. The dreams which came were listless and not of the epoch I was in. I could hear somebody in the room above me – an argument, two men I think. They were arguing. Broken French. Broken English. I couldn't understand it all. Electronic clicking at my ear. The rage of a storm. Rain. A metronome. Fingers at my wrists and neck, checking my pulse. One eyelid lifted, a bright light. A voice barking orders. Mechanical chaos. Hands, so many hands, dragging me from one world into the next, from the land into the water, the deep, deep water.

A gun-shot.

A thud as a body hit the ground.

Blood.

Blood.

Nobody seemed to notice I was singing.

It was something about *goodbye*.

I'm part of you. You are part of me.

***

I awoke sometime in the future. It was night. Without music. I was in the bathroom. In the shower. The water cascaded over me. Blood dripped from two crevices in my forehead but these wounds belonged to somebody else. My fingernails were cracked, chapped, broken. Had I been cast out? If so, from where? By whom?

I stared through the water. Everything appeared fluid, blurry, fashioned of mountainous fractals which had not yet embraced solidity. I was totally disorientated – the water was the only object which seemed sturdy, safe, unyielding and pure. I took deep breaths – it took me more time than I had spare to re-familiarise myself with my surroundings.

The blood…the blood was a message from my former self, of that, I was certain but I wiped it away, it was easy enough in the hot, steaming, water. It didn't mean anything anymore.

I was in pain.

For every reason imaginable.

"Jesus!" I hissed. I had accidently caught a glimpse of myself in the mirrored tiles (most of which were broken and made the reflected image more hideous) and retched. I vomited brown bile into the shower tray. It had been an epoch since I had allowed myself to see myself in such naked *glory*.

I wasn't pretty – I'd be the first to admit it.

For a moment I thought it was someone else bent out of shape, a foetus, under the water but as I moved, I knew it was me – there was the angry pinkish scar which ran from under my neck to my naval where it divided, criss-crossing along my stomach then heading off somewhere around my back, mocking a double-helix as it travelled up my spine. There were those green / brown splotches on the top of my thighs, the mass of almost useless flesh which nestled between my legs – there was more, so much more, but I couldn't look, I couldn't see any more, I'd dreamt enough.

No wonder I had been rejected.

No wonder you wouldn't hold my head when I was sick.

How many times were you going to make me pay for being *me*?

I was all too familiar with the monster I had become – I haunted my own dreams, I was my own nightmare. What had been done to me by myself and others like me over the years – all in the name of *progression*...no, that was wrong...love...it had all been done in the name of love. That's what they said, that's what I told myself.

And my love for him wasn't monstrous, it was angelic...at my lowest points I found humour (and this was one) and laughed at my own pomposity.

I didn't have time for personal reflection; self-conscious navel gazing never got me anywhere. It took me an age but eventually I got to my feet and out of the bathroom. My flesh had more than pruned. I grabbed a towel, dabbed myself dry and dressed. I threw on my jacket, made sure I had the phone and remaining money and headed out.

Downstairs I drifted past the reception desk and remembered that the night manager had told me I was supposed to hand in my key every time I left the hotel but there was nobody there (I did hear some laughter coming from the back room) so it remained in my pocket. I wanted to tell somebody about the gunshot but perhaps that had only been a splinter lost in a whirlwind so praying they yet didn't have surveillance cameras, I rushed down the stairs and out, onto the street.

Sometimes, I truly hate myself.

***

Nobody knew the direction I was heading and that was the fun of the chase.

Across the road, on the pavement, concealed by a bus-stop was a girl and she was watching everything.

She was pretty. Ethereal. I stared back at her through kaleidoscope eyes and pondered for a moment approaching her but the smell of the ocean was in my nostrils and whilst I couldn't see or hear it, I knew it was my guide – I didn't need her. Yes, there was a moon and some stars sprinkled throughout the sky and whilst I did have some basic knowledge of astronomy it wasn't true I could trust the heavens.

The girl raised her hand and waved but I turned my back on her. It wasn't personal. I never communicate with avatars – real or synthetic.

The town was alive and I was grateful. I couldn't have faced it on my own. I drunk it all in: the street full of tea-shops...the post-office...the computer games shop, the store selling sporting goods, the clothes emporiums, the bars, the restaurants...other hotels.

And people.

People everywhere.

People who were alive.

Of course I ignored them all and headed for the main road, which like a spine, ran from one end of the town to the other. There wasn't much traffic (slightly surprising) which meant I was able to cross quickly and safely. I took a breath and headed left. I hadn't walked these pavements in such a long, long time, yet I knew exactly where I was going.

"Is everything okay?" Someone quietly spoke. "Do you need help?" The words brought me back to my senses but I thought they were just a faded memory (from the past or the future I wasn't sure) – I might have imagined them I supposed…I know I didn't…but I might have.

I looked down at my hands – they had already formed into fists. I clenched, unclenched my fingers – I could feel the bones as they cracked. A great pressure fought against my body but I was slow to get going I wasn't going to be defeated.

One foot forward. Then the other. Repeat.

The first. The second. Repeat.

Repeat. Repeat. Repeat.

Within no time I managed to get up a good head of steam.

With the wind behind me, I walked.

No. I didn't need any help.

But I did think it was going to rain.

***

I walked further than planned – I'd even got lost a couple of times which totally fazed me as this was supposed to be a straight road (it certainly used to be) but somehow I had strayed and connected with areas I didn't know. This was disconcerting because everything was true, everything was correct, nothing seemed out of place yet at the same time everything was. There was a thin metallic bench I spied in the distance. When I reached it I sat down to rest and realised that I was outside a small apartment block.

I recognised it immediately.

His apartment block.

This was where he had decided to move following quite a vicious argument with his parents. An old friend (his ex-boyfriend, why are you making me admit that?) had a spare room so he took it (no, I didn't believe they were sleeping together – you might think I was naive but he swore to me that they weren't. I took him at his word). Apparently the rent was peanuts which was all he could afford (that's what he told me but I knew he and his family had plenty of money).

I sat there a long while, though I wasn't sure what I was waiting for. Perhaps I expected him to appear at his door and invite me in or something...it was confusing...lots of noise, emanating from a nearby restaurant.

I glanced over to see if he was there, sitting outside with his friends, eating escargots or steak tartare, washed down with a large glass of Sancerre no doubt.

If he was, I didn't see him.

A bright light shone – I held up my hand to filter most of it out – I preferred dreaming in the darkness. The door to the apartments opened; an old woman filled the frame. She looked familiar but I didn't know from where. She flicked her long blonde hair, fiddled with her glasses. In her arms she held a small yapping dog and I knew that if she didn't get control of it rapidly then it was going to make a bolt for it. It reminded me of Milou from *Tintin*.

I got up as quickly as I could and held the door for her as she had the dog's leash wrapped around the door-handle and the creature was threatened with strangulation or decapitation. Once she had sorted herself out she mumbled thanks (at least I thought it was thanks) and went about her business.

In case she (or anybody else) was watching me, I let the door close but put my foot in the way to stop it shutting completely. The light was extinguished. I took out my phone, pretended I was making a call but the old woman was so caught up with her animal that she never gave me another glance. Thinking it safe, I pushed the door and stepped inside.

I didn't need illumination. I knew everything. I had been here many many times – both in reality and in my mind. This place held dark memories. I stood with the door behind me. To my left was a large mirror which ran the whole length of the corridor; to my right was a collection of post-boxes – ten, twelve, no more. At the far end was an elevator and if I felt like it, a flight of stairs.

There was a rail, I reached out and held it – something at the back of my mind made me nauseous. I remembered helping to carry a sofa up those stairs – a big bright coloured sofa. It was heavy, it weighed a ton. There must have been three, four of us. He was there too and somewhere near the top he had slipped and I'd reached out, grabbed his belt, stopped him from tumbling over – I let that memory go – I didn't know if it was real or imagined even if it was there playing out in my head...

...I was beginning to distrust myself. What was the relevance? The sofa? The colour of it? The people that were there? No, I knew what it was: he didn't need me to help him fall, he did that all by himself.

And once, only once, I wasn't there to catch him...

...how I paid for that for the rest of my life.

Well, up until now perhaps.

***

Lonely. I was so lonely and alone but I ploughed on.

The elevator door screeched as I pulled it open and stepped inside (it reminded me of a large metallic mouth with steel teeth ready to chew me up – an event from my childhood I think). Dust on the buttons. I stared at the numbers – they didn't make sense, I couldn't read them properly. I knew which one I had to press – I had done it so many times.

Second button.

Second floor.

It took an age but the elevator began its ascent. I watched the red arrow - now lit - suggesting we were travelling upwards. When it stopped I didn't move but I had to get out, to see this through to conclusion. All I could think of was home and how I needed to be there right then...I dialled his number in my phone but it was pointless – the signal was dead.

I summoned up enough courage to step out of the elevator and stood directly outside his apartment. There was a bell which I considered ringing but I made a fist and banged on the door's wooden panelling instead.

I was being observed but when I turned my head, nobody was there. I wasn't stupid - they could have been hiding in the shadows, waiting for their opportunity to pounce and do their worst but what would have been the point? The state I was in, what harm did I pose to anybody?

I knocked again. Such acute agony in my knees and ankles. Pain like that I hadn't felt in a long long time.

From the apartment: no answer. If anyone was inside then they were doing a brilliant job of keeping their own counsel. My fingers hovered over the doorbell but there was some...

...one! I forced a smile on my face and turned. "Hello," I muttered, somehow still knowing the language.

***

"Ouch," I then mumbled, reached out for the stairway banister – that pain was worsening (if that was actually possible!).

"There's no-one there," a woman stated the obvious, hands on her hips.

The sweat was dripping down my face. Her expression changed...compassion. "Are you sick? I've got a chair. You want to sit down?"

"No. I'd better go. Thanks." Using the banister I hobbled down the stairs.

"Someone *was* there earlier...an argument. They were shouting loudly. I don't know what it was about. I wasn't listening – but they were very loud. I thought I heard a gunshot...it must have been the television. Or something."

"The walls are quite thin," I offered as an explanation.

"I don't know about that, not exactly, but I heard the door slam – one of them said something about getting some air. They are a strange pair even though I've never seen them. One of them has a lot of visitors." She paused. "There's another guy too. An English guy. Older. He hangs about a lot – sorry, you're English, aren't you? I've seen him, he looks like you – though younger, if you get me. You're looking at me oddly – did I cause offense?"

"No," I lied.

"I don't know what's going on in there so I'm speaking out of turn. They're your friends."

"One of them was and I'm not really sure..." I let my own words trail off.

I had a sudden compunction to tell this woman everything, to explain who I was, where I had come from and why I was there (and yes, I knew who the English guy was, obviously) but she looked bewildered and anyway, I knew the rules...she ended up taking the decision away from me when she closed the door and I could hear voices coming from her apartment - she had guests. They didn't like to be left alone. I continued down the stairs.

When I (eventually) made it to the outside, I took a deep breath – the air seemed much...fresher and things had definitely been...altered. It was hard to put a finger on what had exactly changed but I noticed the differences, subtle though they were. What had before been monochrome was now full colour; where there was once silence there was a symphony of sound. The street, which had been bent out of shape was now straight.

I knew where he had gone or at least where he was heading.

I smiled as I remembered how I loved to dance – I hadn't done it in so long. I don't think I ever danced with you and that was one of the greatest regrets of my life.

I couldn't even breathe when you were around...

***

Violet petals littered the promenade but other than that – the place was empty.

The only sound was the waves as they crashed into the shore. There was a concrete ramp which I climbed down and padded onto the sand. I could see foot-prints, they led directly to the water but I wasn't hundred per cent on that as the sea was outside my range of vision. The salty aroma of the ocean snapped away at my nostrils, like in days gone by.

"Are you there?" I whispered.

Nothing.

I tried again. "If you're there...I have come far to se..."

"Michael."

A voice.

His voice.

It floated. The wind carried it to me. He was here.

"David." My lips formed his name before I said it. "Please...I want...I need to see you."

"I'm not ready."

Along the promenade there was a sudden orchestra of noise: voices, people laughing, shouting, singing. I could hear a carousel too but that possibly came from the other direction. Church bells in the hills rung out. Nothing out of place and yet...

"Where have you been, Michael? I've missed you."

I paused, the sweat poured, making my facade crack. "I've been where I've always been," I replied and that was the truth. It wasn't me who left. "I miss you too...so much...too much probably."

"No," he spat angrily. "You're not being honest, because if you were then I would never have…" His words trailed off.

"Never what? David?"

"It's funny, I'm not sure what I was going to say and isn't that the weirdest thing? I think I was about to tell you something. I think I wanted to tell you everything but now…oh I don't know…"

I sensed he was standing behind me. I turned and smiled. He hadn't changed since that first time I laid eyes on him – though I knew I had. Dramatically.

He had been dressed in his favourite purple suit. It still fitted him so well. His hair had been cut, styled, a slight quiff. His face fresh, only a day or so of stubble. He grinned and I could see his teeth, so white and clean. His shirt was black with two silver skulls on the tips of the collar and around his neck, a tie he had once stolen from me. On his feet he wore a pair of leather boots he had borrowed from his father (and obviously never gave back).

"You look amazing," I whispered. It was true.

"Thank you." He frowned – there was that quizzical expression where he scrunched up his nose and his forehead furrowed.

"I came looking for you," I stated. "I went to the apartment. I spoke to a woman. Your neighbour. She said you were gone. I knew I could find you. I knew you would be here."

"A woman? She sounds kind."

I stepped towards him but he backed away – a mild look of panic – he held up his hand. "It's too early."

I turned back and looked out towards where I imagined those waves to be. I could have sworn that somewhere out there was a light and it was shining...*who will look after me?*

"Did you say something?" David asked. "You can look at me now."

"I'm a little bit frightened," I said. Which was true. I had waited all this time and now I had the opportunity, to look right in his eyes, I couldn't bring myself to do it.

"Frightened?" He burst into laughter. "I've never known you to be frightened of anything."

Ha – if only he knew.

David became serious. "What are you frightened of exactly, Michael?"

"I can't risk losing you again. I can't risk turning around and you're not there, that you are a figment of my imagination and that this, all this, is an illusion and I'll be standing all alone on this beach...if it is a beach. That one day I would never have met you and you asked me to sit down and then..."

David stood beside me. I could smell him. I could smell his cologne. I could smell his shampoo, the wax in his hair. I could smell the lotion on his skin, the deodorant he used.

He rested a finger on my lips. Kept it there for several moments.

He was real.

This wasn't a memory or some voodoo. He was *real*. Even the way he spoke English with that slight American twang – even though he wasn't English nor American.

"I have a question," I began. "I waited at the station. The train station. Earlier. I waited a long time."

"Yes," he replied. "I couldn't come. I wanted to, so much, but I couldn't. Don't be angry. I'm here now. It's just me and that station...well, you know."

"I tried your phone..."

"...phone? Do I still have that?" His enquiry was genuine.

"I went to our bar, you remember the one? I got drunk, things never change, hey?"

A crowd of people drifted along the promenade – I presumed they were making their way to the restaurants and bars of the old port.

"Shall we join them?" He paused. "We used to have a lot of fun didn't we, Michael?" He sounded excited recollecting the past. "But if you rather, we could go to the station – we could sit there and wait for...well, whatever comes along I guess."

"I've checked into a hotel," I stated. "I was supposed to be staying with you in your apartment; that was what was agreed."

"Was it?" he pondered. "I don't think that's possible BUT I could come and stay with you now if you want."

I couldn't help it, I burst into laughter. "That was all I ever wanted. Christ, if only you had said those words to me...

you know…before…"

"I offer you my apologies."

"Forget it. The place I'm staying in though isn't that expensive, it'll do for a night or two."

David stepped closer to the sea. I wanted to grab him, to pull him close, to tell him it was so dangerous out there in the desolate blankness of it all. I wanted him in my arms, his head against my chest where I could make him safe – for the first time though, I wasn't sure that was what he wanted at all. Years ago, if you'd asked me if he wanted us to be together, to stay together forever, I would have answered resolutely yes. But now, worryingly, I wouldn't have known what the answer would have been.

***

"Everyone said I'd been a dick to you, and you know what? They were right." David sounded contrite but then he changed direction. "I used to talk about the void a lot didn't I? Ironic now, considering."

"There was a time when you spoke of nothing else."

He scratched under his eye. "I don't want to be melancholic but I have to tell you this – I dreamt about it the other day. The first time in a long while. I can't shake the image – that image of total nothingness. It's been playing on my mind.

I heard a voice..."

"The other day?" Now this intrigued me. "When exactly?"

"...I'm not sure exactly. Yesterday? The day before...I don't suppose it matters."

"What DO you remember, then?"

David threw himself into my arms. I caught him. He wrapped his legs around me. "I don't want to talk about it. I'm so happy to see you. I'm so happy you're here. I'm so happy you came back to me." He beamed. "Let's walk together, like we used to? I'll let you hold my hand – will you kiss me Michael... tell me you love me."

I let him out of my arms gently, his eyes were innocent, so inquisitive – I remembered I wanted to see the world through those eyes.

"David, we can do whatever you want."

He nodded furiously. "It's exactly what I want. What I always wanted. I know sometimes I was bad to you. I know I slept with people behind your back...I couldn't...oh, I don't know, it all sounds so insignificant now doesn't it? I loved you. I love you. I always did."

I held out my hand. He grabbed it. Mine seemed still so much larger than his. I gave it a squeeze. "Which way would you like to go?"

"Along the water's edge – we did that a lot didn't we?"

"I think you might have, I'm not sure that *we* did. And, we certainly didn't hold hands."

"A shame. But we are now, aren't we?"

"You used to go walking at some very strange hours – there was this one time, I think we must have argued about something trivial, I can't quite remember, but anyway you walked for over two hours up and down the coastline. You said you even headed up to the mountains. I don't know what you were looking for or if you ever found it."

"Ha! That does sound like me doesn't it?" He prodded the side of his head. "Sometimes there was so much noise going on in here that it was deafening. I had to get away, go to places where I was alone, the only one, and I could hear were the sounds of the universe around me rather than the world inside me. I would be lucky sometimes and the noise inside would be drowned out and I'd go home happy."

"Let's try this way," I suggested, pulling him along with me.

***

"You look as if you have something on your mind?" I asked after a while. We had walked far along the beach, through the dunes – we still held hands.

"I'm not sure...I don't think so...not really. I suppose I'm finding a lot of this strange."

"That goes for two of us."

"I was thinking about the old port...it was true we used to have a lot of fun but the bars, the clubs, they seem so empty..." How lost he sounded.

"If we could have been together...before today...well, I would have been here."

"I said to you so many times all you had to do was ask me, I would never have left, I would have come back."

"You wanted me to make the decision for you?"

"Well, you did do that in the end didn't you?"

There was a silence which I found uncomfortable. "All I'm saying David is that I just wanted you to want me the way I wanted you. I would have done anything..."

He faced me; put a finger on my lips. "Did you ever fall in love again?"

I held his hand tighter. "It took me a long time to admit my love for you. You changed a lot of things about me. I never regret meeting you."

"You didn't answer my question but listen, I wouldn't be angry if you did fall in love with someone else...well, not too angry."

"David, you were the love of my life. I told you so many times. It wasn't a lie. I never lied to you. It was the truth even if I wasn't the love of your life. That hurt, of course it did, but I grew to accept it." I took a deep breath. "Sometimes there was more than the physical distance between us, did you ever feel it? We could be in the same room, lying next to each other, yet at the same time we seemed so far apart."

"What do you mean?!" He sounded genuinely offended. "You know how I felt about you!"

"It wasn't the same."

"Forgive me," he whispered eventually.

"It's not important anymore."

"No. It is. I pushed you away, like I do everybody."

"We can agree on that."

"You stuck around the longest though." He chuckled but there was no mirth. "I know I hurt you."

"Don't worry…I'm here…"

"Together again. Forever and always."

"If that is what you want."

"I promise Michael, I won't ever leave you."

"Better not make promises you can't keep."

"I think the truth of the situation is I couldn't even if I wanted to."

David was right, and that was the point.

That was the actual point of all this.

If the experiment worked, of course and all this wasn't just fantasy.

***

"Oh, do you think we can go back to your hotel?"

As we walked we held hands so tightly. I didn't want to let him go and I convinced myself it was the same for him.

It was a balmy night but neither of us felt the cold.

"I'd like that very much," I started. "But somehow I think it might be a mistake. Perhaps next time."

"It upset you that I slept with other men didn't it? Will you always hold it against me?"

I carefully chose my response. "What hurt me was that I was the one who loved you the most yet you wouldn't sleep with me. There were times we partied and other guys would paw you, prod you, caress you and ultimately fuck you and you never said a word – yet me, the one who adored you with all my heart, my whole heart, you wouldn't go near. If I touched you, you'd make that face of pure disgust and smack me away. It hurt me then. It hurts me now."

I could tell that my words had made an impact. "Once you asked me to be your boyfriend. You wanted us to be in a couple." David started. "We were in the karaoke bar…" He paused as he was obviously reliving it too. "We were drinking. We were having fun. We were writing notes to each other on tiny pieces of paper."

"That's right."

"You asked me if we could be together. You said that you loved me and said that we should be together. I said no."

"You broke my heart."

"I told you that we should be friends. The best of friends."

"I agreed that being friends was better than nothing but perhaps I should have walked out of that bar and your life. Perhaps it would have been better all round."

He scratched his forehead. "Do you want to know why I said no?"

"You had your reasons."

David stopped walking. "I was nervous."

"Of what? Even though at that point we'd only known each other a couple of months and had met only a handful of times there was such a deep connection between us. Everybody saw it. Everybody said so."

"And that was part...there was...too much...pressure."

"It was because I was older. You couldn't accept the age difference between us...but did that really matter? When we were together we were great..."

"It did...but not probably for the reasons you're thinking."

I could feel old anger rising, had to hold my temper. I didn't want to argue.

"Michael, I had problems with your age in terms of the years between us and what they represented. I know you found it annoying when we went out and people thought you were my father."

"I'm not sure I want to be reminded."

"It embarrassed you and on their behalf, I'm sorry. I loved it though – I loved the fact that people thought you could be responsible for me. That you were someone who was capable of creating me. That was so profoundly attractive. My parents were bastards but you came along in my life when I was feeling unloved and you made me feel…you made me want to live, to stay alive…you know? You picked me Michael, you picked me."

"That's the nicest thing you've ever said."

"I know I should have said it properly before, perhaps with more clarity or honesty. I loved you more than I loved anybody else."

"Just not enough for us to be together."

There was water on his cheek. Was that a tear? "You being older reminded me of my own mortality. Say we had got together then what would we have had? Ten, fifteen years maybe?"

"Some people don't even get that."

"If we were going to be together, I wanted more, Michael. With you, I wanted always and forever. What you could offer me then wasn't enough."

David kicked sand into the air as he stormed away. "Never forget that I love you but there were some things that I just couldn't…just couldn't do. I could never stand over your corpse…" His words choked him, he ceased talking. He fell to the ground, drew his legs up under his chin, rocked backwards and forwards. I realised he was humming.

I wanted to sit next to him, to put an arm around him, to tell him that everything was going to be okay but I knew if I did that then I would be false.

I had to accept that he did love me, just in his own way, that was always the truth of it – but now I was here with him again, the other times came bleeding through my synapses: the arguments, the bitterness, the betrayals. Things hadn't been right for a while and I think that he was starting to remember them too.

We would have to work through them...

"Perhaps you shouldn't have come," he whispered as he rubbed his eyes.

"Where else would I have gone?"

He lay back on the sand, stretched out his limbs. "You look different to how I imagined."

That much was true. "It's been twenty years since...since I was last here."

"Twenty years? Then, you don't look half bad."

"You're a good liar."

"I've been doing it my whole life."

***

"...understood it wasn't easy?" David started.

"What do you mean?"

"You know...after I...I died?"

So he knew something of what had happened? They would be interested to know that. The people here were...self aware?

"I don't think we should talk about it," I replied.

He raised his head. "But that's why you're here, isn't it? You're looking for some reasoning? About what happened. About what I did to myself." David got to his knees, ran his hand through the sand then opened his fingers so it floated away on the light breeze, a breeze that I felt on my cheeks. "I used to love to sleep all the time because when I dreamt, I dreamt of you and I felt that if I...if I embraced the void then we would have been together forever. Warped way of thinking, hey?"

"I've never stopped thinking about you," I whispered.

"There's never been another?" He pushed once more.

"Not like you. You were everything I ever wanted."

"I'm sorry for what I did...to us...to myself...I went too far. I should never have taken those pills, I should never have run that bath...I should never have...it was my brother's gun..."

"...don't David."

"Do you think we could have been happy together. If we'd tried? If I'd tried?" He was staring at me with a look of such want, of such need, sculptured into his features. "We will never know for certain," I started. "But why not?"

From somewhere across the ocean came the sound of the semantron. He jumped up, shook the sand from the pockets of his suit. "One of us has to leave," he stated.

"It's calling me. I'd better go back to the hotel and get ready."

"Will the sun ever rise again for us?"

"I hope so David, I hope so."

"And you will come back?"

"Would you like me too?"

"I...I'd like it very much."

"Where will you go now?"

David pointed vaguely in the direction towards the sea. "Down there somewhere. Amongst the crabs."

I nodded, started to walk away.

"Michael," he called.

"Yes, David?"

"Never say goodbye, au revoir yes, but never goodbye. You once did say it to me and well, that was the end of things, wasn't it?"

I headed up the concrete steps and back onto the promenade. I didn't look back. I pulled up my collar and took a leisurely stroll back to the hotel. I felt like it was twenty years ago. I was happy.

My feet knew the way. I didn't have to direct them.

The rain, if it came, I ignored it.

***

A lways…

It was chilly at the train station the following morning. The wind was building; I knew I didn't have long. Though that was okay, there was no need for me to be here any longer. What needed to be said had been. I walked onto the platform. The train was there, waiting. I went to step on but stopped. I knew he was behind me. I felt his hand on my shoulder. His mouth was at my ear. "We promised didn't we… never ever say goodbye. Au revoir, always."

"I'll see you soon. I promise. You asked me to come back, so I will."

I climbed aboard. David stayed on the platform. I put my luggage in the rack and found my seat easily. I removed my jacket and settled back – I had a long journey before me.

As the train pulled away I thought for a moment about the time I had said goodbye, about the time I left him on the platform crying – that hadn't been my intention obviously, I had said goodbye as a matter of course, I didn't realise how vulnerable he was – he took my words to heart. He went to his ex-boyfriend's place, he ran a bath, he took some pills; he used the gun his broth-er hid under the bed. Nobody told me for three months what had happened. He was the love of my life and he broke my heart. Twice.

I never forgave myself.

I should never have left him.

I should never have left you.

But I made myself a promise. I created the technology. I swore to myself – if I could go back, I would.

I was the first, a pioneer some might say, and many would follow.

In my heart of hearts I knew I would see David again, if I, if he, wanted it enough. And right now it seemed he did. Our bond was too powerful.

I closed my eyes and let the train do the work – on the platform, David danced.

I swore I would never say goodbye again.

***

...and forever.

I wasn't on the train when I came too and perhaps, I never really had been. I let the others disconnect me from the wires, the cables, the probes and electrodes. I climbed out of the machine, coughed up a mouthful of blood (not that that was unusual for me anymore), collected my clothes and headed to the door.

The nurse held out her hand to guide me.

"I hope everything was to your satisfaction, sir."

I smiled, I actually felt it was.

I had never felt so...alive.

I nodded.

"Then you can ask of yourself no more," she said enigmatically.

The door was closed behind me and I left the sound of the semantron echoing somewhere in the distance – it called other travellers now. The room I found myself in was full of people, and for once, some called me friend…the best of friends…

…I heard a voice.

And that voice was you.

BIOGRAPHIES

Allen Ashley is a British Fantasy Award winning editor and a prize-winning poet. He is the author or editor of 14 published books, the most recent of which is an updated, revised version of his novel "The Planet Suite" (Eibonvale Press, UK, 2016). He is the sole judge for the annual British Fantasy Society Short Story Competition. He works as a critical reader and a creative writing tutor, with five groups currently running across north London. His next project will be "Humanagerie" – an anthology he is co-editing with Sarah Doyle for Eibonvale Press. www.allenashley.com

Adrian Chamberlin was born in Wales and lives in Oxfordshire. He is the author of the critically acclaimed supernatural thriller "The Caretakers" as well as numerous short stories in a variety of anthologies, mostly historical or futuristic based supernatural horror. He edited the supernatural warfare novella collection "Darker Battlefields", released by The Exaggerated Press in summer 2016 and has many more projects in the pipeline.

Adrian Cole is a native and resident of Devon. Adrian has had some two dozen novels and many short stories published, some also as ebooks and audio books over the last 40 years. He writes SF, fantasy and horror, and "Nick Nightmare Investigates" - featuring his laconic, hard-boiled occult private eye, Nick Nightmare - won the British Fantasy Society Award for the Best Collection of 2015. His short stories have appeared in Year's Best anthologies and he is a regular contributor to magazines such as Weirdbook, Cirsova and Occult Detective Quarterly. His most recent book is "Tough Guys", published by Parallel Universe Publications (UK).

Leah Crowley is an award-winning author, poet and lyricist. During her spare time she campaigns for equal rights. Her literary works have also been featured on the BBC and other popular media outlets. Leah began to take an interest in writing and creativity from the age of six. Currently she is working on several projects including "Battle Hymns", a collection of poetry themed around historical events and battles. In her spare time she studies piano and repeatedly listens to music from

Liberace to Modern Talking, Lady Gaga, Elton John to Kylie Minogue. Leah is a makeup addict and enjoys shopping, eating out and drinking lots of coffee.

Dean M. Drinkel is an award winning scriptwriter, director and author. He divides his time between Cannes, France and Kent, England.

Stephanie Ellis writes speculative fiction stories which have found success in a variety of horror magazines and anthologies. Her first novella, "Domnuill-dhu", has recently been published in Dark Chapter Press's "Bloody Heather" anthology. She is also co-editor at The Infernal Clock and at Trembling with Fear, the online magazine branch of Horror Tree (the online writer's resource). She is currently awaiting decisions from publishers following submission of a novel and a novella. Samples of her writing can be found on http://stephellis.weebly.com/ and she is on twitter at @el_stevie.

Cate Gardner is a British horror author with over a hundred short stories published. Most recently, her work has appeared in The Dark, Black Static, Postscripts, Sherlock Holmes's School for Detection, and has been twice nominated for the British Fantasy Award. Forthcoming for 2018 is inclusion in Paula Guran's "Year's Best Dark Fantasy & Horror 2017" and Stephen Jones' "The Mammoth Book of Halloween

Stories". You can find her on the web at www.categardner.net.

Marie O'Regan is an award-nominated author and editor. She has released two collections of short fiction, "Mirror Mere" and "In Times of Want", as well as many short stories, a novelette ("Curse of the Ghost"), a novella ("Bury Them Deep"), and has edited the anthologies: "Hellbound Hearts", "The Mammoth Book of Body Horror", "The Mammoth Book of Ghost Stories by Women", and "Carnivale: Dark Tales from the Fairground". Her genre journalism has appeared in magazines like The Dark Side, Rue Morgue and Fortean Times, and her interview book with prominent figures from the horror genre, "Voices in the Dark", was released in 2011. Her short fiction has been published in the US, UK, Germany and Italy, and she is Co-Chair of the UK Chapter of the Horror Writers' Association. Marie is represented by Jamie Cowen of The Ampersand Agency.

Steven Savile has written for *Doctor Who*, *Torchwood*, *Primeval*, *Stargate*, *Warhammer*, *Slaine*, *Fireborn*, *Pathfinder*, *Arkham Horror*, *Rogue Angel*, and other popular game and comic worlds. He won the International Media Association of Tie-In Writers award for his novel, "Shadow Of The Jaguar", and the inaugural Lifeboat to the Stars Award from for "Tau Ceti" (co-authored with International Bestselling novelist Kevin J. Anderson). Writing as Matt Langley his young adult novel "Black Flag" was a finalist for the People's Book Prize 2015. He wrote the story for the multi-million copy bestselling computer game *Battlefield 3* and has worked with Paradox Interactive on several of their forthcoming computer games. His latest books include "Sherlock Holmes And The Murder At Sorrows Crown", published by Titan in 2016, "Parallel Lines" a brand new crime novel from the same publisher in 2017, and "Glass Town", a mythic fantasy novel published in hardcover by St Martin's Press also in 2017.

Phil Sloman is a writer of dark fiction. His novella "Becoming David" was shortlisted for a British Fantasy Society Best Newcomer award in 2017. Phil likes to peak behind the curtain of reality and see what might be lurking there. Sometimes he writes down what he sees. His short stories which can be found throughout various anthologies. In the humdrum of everyday life, Phil lives with an understanding wife and a trio of vagrant cats who tolerate their human slaves. There are no bodies buried beneath the patio as far as he is aware. Occasionally Phil can be found lurking here: http://insearchofperdition.blogspot.co.uk/ or wasting time on Facebook – come say hi.

Lightning Source UK Ltd.
Milton Keynes UK
UKHW021153020819
347284UK00006B/218/P